I0723234

# BOYS BUY ME DRINKS TO WATCH ME FALL DOWN

## AND OTHER STORIES

ANNA DICKSON JAMES

WHISKEY TIT

NYC & VT

This is a work of fiction. Names, characters, places, and incidents are the product of the author's imagination, and should not be confused with your idea of reality.

Resemblance to actual persons, living or dead, events, or locales is entirely coincidental.

Published in the United States and Canada by Whisk(e)y Tit: www.whiskeytit.com. If you wish to use or reproduce all or part of this book for any means, please let the author and publisher know. You're pretty much required to, legally.

ISBN 978-1-952600-33-3

Copyright ©2023, the author. All rights reserved.

Cover art by Eric Pardue.
Cover design by Brian Pickens.

*For Sonora and Shelby —*

*my bright and beautiful girls*

# CONTENTS

# INTRODUCTION

*By Allison Moore*

"Where had I gone?"

It's a disquieting question, one that embodies the unnerving feeling of not recognizing yourself, or your surroundings. The title character in "Proud to be a Shriner's Wife" actually voices this question, and that sense of self-estrangement and displacement pervades the entirety of Anna Dickson James' stellar collection.

These stories map the jagged, lopsided topography of relationships between women and men, mothers and children. I found myself reading the stories compulsively, sometimes furtively. Why? Because I felt so exposed.

I'm an educated professional. A happily married feminist. A responsible parent. People tell me I'm both competent and sane.  I'm not the kind of woman who's supposed to gauge everything I say and do by a mental calculus that factors in everyone else first. Except that I do.  I usually console myself with the thought that no one else could possibly know the extent of my neurosis, until I read this collection.

Story after story gave me the uneasy feeling that I'd been outed, my secret anxiety and exhaustion laid bare. The emotional computations of the characters are constant, a steady drone that directs them to accommodate everyone, as much as possible, all the time.

And the women in these stories don't just accommodate their husbands or their children. They are compelled to accommodate other people's children, pets they clearly stated they did not want, even a stranger who takes an adjoining seat on a train — indeed, even when the stranger draws blood.

In real life, the unceasing compulsion to at least consider everyone else's wants and needs can easily — often mercifully — become white noise. The background hum we ignore. In her precise, unflinching prose, Dickson James amplifies this white noise until it becomes a signal insisting that we hear it.

At times, it's mortifying. That's by design. It's uncomfortable to watch a breast cancer survivor put up with a self-absorbed partner. Irritating to realize the bone-tired waitress at the music festival will dutifully help her roadie boyfriend hump cable to the truck at the end of a very long night. Painful to watch the ultimate cool girl awkwardly navigate an unexpected pregnancy with her maddeningly woke boyfriend.

And then there's the sex. A lot of sex, of all different kinds. The cringeworthy variety (when sweet talk consists of a partner declaring, "I feel like I'm screwing a corpse."). The careful-what-you-wish-for type (when a truly erotic threesome starts in a bed of tomato plants). The please-sweet-Jesus-save-her kind (when a very drunk woman is escorted to her hotel room by a stranger, and both the woman and the reader have to examine what our general expectations of men should be).

And then there's "The Rapture of Anne Marie Abbot," which – trust me – you just have to read, because I can't unpack everything in there about female desire and faith and shame and spiritual ecstasy.

To paraphrase the "Sommelier Mort Vivant," even when it's embarrassing, Dickson James tells the truth. The miracle is that she tells it with incredible tenderness.

Her sensitivity extends to the men who populate her stories as well. They are bewildered and lonely, controlling and ashamed. Angry at times, but rarely mean. Mostly, what they want is comfort, a time and place where no one needs anything from them.

In "The Easy Chair," the protagonist has become so genuinely overwhelmed, his nerves so frayed from the simple daily demands of work and relationships that he throws himself into an obsessive quest to create the perfect massage chair—with hilarious and alarming results. And we can't help but root for the aging agoraphobe bachelor who accidentally receives an enormous piñata and a mountain of party favors, as this quirk of the universe causes him to reconsider his otherwise controlled life.

I first heard the term "emotional labor" during the pandemic lockdown. Oxford offers a pretty good definition:

**emotional labor**, noun. The mental activity required to manage or perform the routine tasks necessary for maintaining relation-ships and ensuring smooth running of a household or process, typically regarded as an unappreciated or unacknowledged burden borne disproportionately by women. – Oxford Languages Dictionary

By turning up the volume on the soundtrack of emotional labor, Dickson James affirms its existence – for all her characters, men and women, and even for competent, sane feminists.

Yes, it's terrifying to feel exposed. But it's also a relief to be recognized. And know you are not alone.

*January 2023*

*Allison Moore is a writer for stage, television and feature films, including the upcoming Disney Animation Studios feature, <u>Wish</u> ('23).*

# THE ART OF DROWNING

Smile at the husband. Smile at him because he will bring home the oysters I like to eat. Smile at him and cook his dinner. Slide into his bed with bare legs and one arched eyebrow because then he will be content to read his paper and leave me alone. When it goes too long without, he starts to pick at me about the shells, talk to me about the sand always on the floor, and the wet, musty smell in the towels.

Be kind to the baby. Feed it when it cries. Change it. Coo to it. Smile. It too likes when I smile. I walk with it on my hip until its arms grow limp and its head settles onto my shoulder. When the baby sleeps, a low growl comes from the back of its throat. Because of the noise, I sit at its crib and watch and wait for it to stir.

The baby bangs a glass ashtray on a glass table. I sit on the husband's green couch and watch the news. A mother cat raced into a burning building seven times to bring out seven babies. It lost an eye, and the fire melted the mother's face leaving a gaping, lopsided jaw. The mother cat's whiskers are off. Fur singed. In my peripheral vision I notice the baby sucking on a copper penny.

The husband bursts through the front door. The walls startle, and plaster falls down in little ticks at his feet. He is carrying a small box. I move to the fireplace and arrange the shells that sit on our mantle.

"Hi," the husband says.

I look past him towards the open door.

He picks up the copper penny baby.

"Hi, Little One," he says. And then he frowns.

"What's in your mouth?" he asks and fishes inside.

He finds the coin. The baby gags. And then coos. The baby moves quickly from gagging to cooing, from crying to laughing.

"Oh my God. A penny," the husband says and rubs the wet coin on his pants.

"Oh my God," I say.

"Christ, Emily. You have to be more careful."

"My name is Elizabeth," I say under my breath.

"What?" the husband says.

The husband drops the coin into his pocket. I put a shell to my ear and listen to the ocean waves trapped inside.

"I have to be more careful," I say.

The baby wiggles to be let down, and the husband lets it go. He splashes his face with water from the kitchen sink and dries off with a paper towel. He leans his back on the countertop and crosses arms in front of him and looks at me sideways.

"How was your day…" he pauses and adds, "… Emily."

He knows I've come to hate that name, but he is testing me. I turn away from him and put the shell on the mantle, slide it a little to the right so that the end is pointing towards the open window, towards its ocean home.

I do not want to go back to the hospital, so I bare my right shoulder, look over it towards him and say, "I missed you."

The husband uncrosses his arms and walks over to me. His hair looks and smells like black copier ink. He puts his hands square on my shoulders and hesitating, kisses my cheek. When I lean in, he lets out a long breath, and his hands are already groping under my shirt. He is a greedy man.

The baby cries. I bend down to it and pick it up, and the baby leans in and nuzzles my breast.

"There, there," I say to it, and I give it a cold bottle right from the fridge. The baby whines at first but then begins to gulp and slurp. The baby is greedy too.

The husband hands me the velvet box he brought in. I sit on the green couch, prop the baby up with his bottle, and open the gift. It is a perfect circle made of polished abalone.

"Abalone," I say.

The husband tries so hard.

"You love things from the sea," the husband tells me.

"Yes," I say, and because it's something my twin would have done, I put my head on the husband's shoulder. He watches the baby drink, and I watch the gulls circle outside my window. I see their beaks open to cry, but through the thick pane, I hear nothing.

When the boat went down, I saw my sister gripping the red cooler as it bobbed on the pulling tide. I tried to swim toward her, but the waves and the rain and the cold of the water held me steady, and she floated farther and farther away from me. We had identical hair, identical bodies, identical clothing. She looked just like me, floating away from me.

Water seeped into my nose, my throat, burning, muscles cramping, but I tried to reach her. I stopped to rest by lying on my back, letting the water hold me up. Thick clouds, pushed by the wind, tumbled in front of the darkened sun. When I drew my head up again, Emily was gone. Though the beach sat impossibly small and distant on the horizon, I kicked and pawed towards the shore. I began to sink. Three feet. Four feet. Five. I made one last effort to aim and push in the direction of the speckled light as the sea's swirling water began to sing a syncopated lullaby.

The sun's light funneled smaller and smaller above me. Sea dust and flotsam began to collect in the fan of my red hair. I sank down into the sandy bottom of the sea, stretched out like I was relaxing on the couch after a particularly hard day at work.

My pale arms took on the ocean's green tint. I sifted the sand through my fingers, let the last bit of air trickle out of my mouth. My last breath's bubble caught on the tip of my lashes. I blinked to let it go.

I hoped it was the same for Emily.

The doctors believe they have it figured out, but they don't know. She was always the better half of me.

Though we had the same eyes, the same sloped nose, the identical gait and walk, she was still somehow prettier. Her hair shone brighter; her eyes lit easier. She was smarter and more likable too. Emily has a husband and a child who needs her. I have only me needing me. It's natural they'd prefer her to me.

The stethoscope. The metal bedframe. The thick mashed potatoes and the spoon that went with it. At the hospital they keep everything cold. That's why the crazies wear knit caps indoors. It's the sanest thing they do. For 45 minutes twice a day, they'd tend to me, but I spent most of my time avoiding the drifters, the screamers, the ladies and grown men that cried and moaned from the time they got up to the time they took their sedatives. When the doctors did come to me, they had me practice writing her name. *Emily. Emily. Emily.* The first few weeks I refused. I'd make a big curlicue show of writing an "E" but my hand could not help pulling the ink to the "l" to the "i" to the "z."  They would warn me then with a parental frown.

"Eeeeemmmilyyyy," they'd say, drawing it out long and low in the tone I'd used on my yellow lab when he'd shit on the rug.

"You can go home as soon as you learn your name," the nurses would say, until, finally, I gave in.

"Emily," I said. The nurse on duty applauded and said, "Wait right here."

She came back grinning, with a clipboard in her hand, the supervisor at her side.

"What is your name, Honey?" the nurse asked.

Look at the nurse. Smile at the nurse. Answer the nurse with my sister's name.

"Emily," I say.

"What's your husband's name?"

Answer the nurse though it feels adulterous and shameful.

"Sean," I say.

"What's your baby's name?"

"Sean," I say again.

The nurses do not try to hide their excitement.

"You must miss them," the supervisor says. "Would you like me to call them?"

"Yes," I say.


Both Seans come to visit that afternoon. The nurses have combed my hair and let me wear a cardigan the mother brought in for me when I was still Elizabeth. I put it on over the hospital gown. The plastic tag, still in place, scratches at my neck.

"Emily?" the husband asks.

I nod.

"Thank God you're back," the big Sean says and puts the baby in my lap.

The baby looks at me blankly, and I think he is the only one who understands. While I am contemplating this, he reaches up and puts his fingers in my mouth.

"Num, Num," I say, and I pretend to nibble on his hands. It's a game we used to play when I was still me.

In two weeks, they let me go home to my sister's house, to my sister's life. All I had to do was agree to be her.

My pupils are large and eat the light they gather, and this makes the husband uncomfortable. So I keep the sand swept up and his collared shirts ironed in a row in his closet. I keep pennies away from the baby. I wear the black bra that opens in the front, remove the washer from the kitchen faucet so I can hear the water drip. As a penance I go to visit my sister every day.

"Emily," the mother says and hugs me.

"I'm Elizabeth," I confide in a whisper.

"Sssssh," she says. "We'll have none of that talk today."

"Here is my scar," I whisper again and point to my forehead. "I fell off the bed when I was five. Don't you remember?"

The mother begins to cry and says, "Emily fell off the bed."

"I fell off the bed," I say.

"Would you like some lunch?" the mother says.

"Yes," I say.

The mother fixes me a plate of tuna salad with a side of pickled beets. Like the husband, she is always testing me. Emily would eat the beets, but I leave them on my plate.

"Don't you want your beets?" the mother prods.

"You know I hate them," I say.

The mother sighs and says, "Go take your swim. I'll watch the baby."

Surf flushes in and out of the tide pool until the water recedes. Stranded sea stars dry in the afternoon sun, waiting for the gulls to come. I carefully pry them from the rocks, gather them in my satchel and walk into the sea. Soon my legs lift off the ground, and I push out past the breaking waves. I dive down and one by one place the sea stars on the sandy floor where their missing limbs will grow back. I stay down as long as I can, lingering in the quiet noise the ocean makes, feeling at home. In the bubbling tide, I hear my sister call out my name.

"Elizabeth, Elizabeth," she says.

I find her at low tide, sitting at the ocean floor, atop her cooler, wearing my old body. The water moves the collar of her shirt, fluttering open and shut, revealing and hiding the slope of her still chest.

The baby is in the tub. Splash. Splash. The water says my true name. Do not take off my shirt. Do not take off my socks. Sink low into the tub. Dip my hair under while the baby sits on my stomach, gurgling. Make sure to get out before the husband sees.

Put his casserole in the oven. Hang his crisp, white shirts on the line. Add a can of anchovies and an opener to the cooler I keep hidden in the basement. Look in the mirror to brush my hair. Notice the scar is fading.

The mother comes again.

"Go on, Emily," she says, and Elizabeth goes.

I pick the sea stars off the stones like sticky, hard shelled grubs. Swim out to the sea where my sister waits. She rises from her plastic chair and walks to me. I open my mouth to let the water in. My lungs bulge and sag with new weight, and I sink to the ocean floor. I reach out and touch Emily's feet. Manicured and perfect, her skin is white and puffed along the nails' edge.

We sit cross legged, knees touching, hands clasped. Nothing moves but the tips of our red hair, rising naturally towards the surface of the water.

Emily begins to cough, and bubbles slip out from between her lips in delicate gags. I watch as they float to the water's surface. Emily chokes on the next wave of air as it is born from somewhere inside of her. Round circles of breath tumble out from her gaping mouth.

A sharp pain penetrates my shoulder, and a red gash rips across Emily's forehead. My sister begins to kick towards the surface, blood and bubbles surround her head like a crown. Four feet from where my sister surfaces, a boat's black shadow appears, blocking out the sun's perfect orb.

Cotton headed and drowsy, I lie my head on the sandy bottom. My abalone necklace pulls away from my neck and settles softly in the sand. A giant clam yawns, revealing her pearl. She too is tired and calls me to pluck the pain from her mouth. I twist the pearl from its rubber home and swallow it like a gemstone pill.

"It's good medicine," I say, and the clam sings a watery dirge.

Sea stars gather with their wounded limbs and bid me to rest.

"Wait," I tell them. I watch to see Emily's perfect feet, her beautiful hair, all of the good that was better than me, lifted out of the water and disappear into the side of a fisherman's boat.

I nod, and the sea stars attach themselves to my shoulders and back like a blanket. They form a new skin that thickens and hardens, sealing the soft part of me inside. I become the pearl I ate, the sister I could not let go.

# 2

# SOMMELIER MORT VIVANT

When the guys and I started prowling around down-town, we'd eat any brain we came across. The neighbor-hood grocer, a med student coming off her rounds, a kid on his way to baseball practice. Didn't really matter. A brain is a brain is a brain. Or so we thought.

But here's the truth, if you really want to know it: smarter brains taste better. There's an undeniable quality to a taught, exercised hypothalamus bathed in juicy neurons. If a Second Lifer has trained her palate, she can taste the quality of a person's thoughts and ideas. So me and the boys, we started hanging around universities and hospitals, which didn't guarantee a smarter brain, but the likelihood did go up.

I know what you're thinking. You see us "zombies" cracking skulls like walnuts, munching away like animals, and how could we really get the taste of a brain with all the little bits of bone, pieces of skin, hair, and doesn't that dilute the meat? And well, we thought of that too, so when you see the ones on the street eating the brains outright, you can go ahead and call them the zombies because they don't know any better. But us Second Lifers, we take the time to do it right. We crack the skull clean, section out the cerebellum, the thalamus, save the pituitary gland like my grandmother saved the "chestnut" from the turkey, a soft little nugget of meat above the wishbone. We set up a table, eat it with a knife and fork.

I used to think sommeliers were racket artists, which is to say that I used to think my husband was a con. He was obsessed with his collection, arranging the wines by type and year, spending money that we could have used for vacations or to get a new water heater so I could take a hot shower longer than 5 minutes. He'd open a bottle and sniff the cork, and immediately my eyes would roll. I couldn't help it. He'd discuss the woodsy flavor, like oak, no- like birch with hints of cherry

Know what he never said? Subtle notes of grape.

But now that I'm a connoisseur in my own right, I get it. The brain of a 7-year-old is different from the brain of an 82-year-old, and the thalamus of an engineer is different from the thalamus of a slaughterhouse worker.

And the grey matter of a creative? They have so many strange neural pathways, basting and marinating all day long in electrical pulses. I ate the brain of a sculptor once, and I don't know if it's because he was a reader (there were books all along his shelves) or because he worked in a 3 D medium, but he was so tender, so juicy, tangy like liver. I could taste the blood, the trace amounts of lead and alcohol, but I could also taste how his fingertips felt on the clay.

So now I fancy myself a sort of sommelier mort vivant. I feel like a douche bag even saying it, but it's true, you know. And even when it's embarrassing, I tell the truth. I was never one to allow myself to feel good about myself, but when you're dead and you have nothing else to lose, things become clearer, and you don't really mind seeing things for what they are or what they were in your previous life. I guess I should say I don't really mind seeing things for what they were in MY previous life. The one in which I was a wife to a good man and a mother to a 4-month-old baby girl.

So anyways, when me and the boys go out to prowl, I tell them who we're going to hit. They pretty much do as I ask, and I'm kind of their leader because without me, they'd still be eating politician brains, if you know what I mean. I know that joke is low hanging fruit, but I have yet to eat a mayor's brain that's been as succulent as a high school English teacher's. The world should know.

As a Second Lifer, I'm trying to detect subtle differences in brain taste and texture between men and women, between ethnicities, between those who are formally educated and those who are not. (You can take the woman out of the lab, but you can't take the lab out of the woman.) But in my research, as objective as one can be when it comes to something as subjective as taste, none of those factors matter. The only variable that counts is intelligence.

Bob, one of the dumbest and most superstitious of us in the group, swears that he could taste more "Cajun" when we were in New Orleans trying to find a priestess to make us First Life again, but Bob also thinks that green M&M's make him horny.

Bob is my boyfriend now. I met him in the herd outside of town. He was sucking on the tail of a rat, leaving the best, brainy part for last. He gnawed up to the belly, and he was going at it so wholeheartedly, over a scrawny rat, I figured that this guy must have a unique optimism or a reservoir of pleasure that I desperately needed. He noticed me staring and mistook my interest for hunger, and he offered me the rest. I said, "Yes," we went on a few dates, yadda, yadda, yadda. But thank God nothing makes Bob horny any more.

My husband used to come up behind me when I was at the kitchen sink doing dishes. He'd nuzzle his nose in my hair, press himself against the back of my thigh, and it really used to knock me out, the smell of him, the feel of him against me. I left the dishes for the morning more often than not, when I was married.

But with Bob, I don't know if I could do it. It's bad enough I gotta' listen to my bones rattle down the street, and bad enough I gotta' eat the brains of probably good and decent people, and bad enough that I've learned the zombie body rots just as much as the First Life body breaks down, and then I gotta' listen to Bob prattle on about ghosts and werewolves as if they were real, and watch him gobble up his meals without using a napkin, without taking the time to really enjoy the crisp crackle of a spinal cord severing.

Bob wants to know why I'm not researching a cure to Second Life, but to be honest, and again, I'm always being honest, a cure doesn't really interest me. What am I going to do if I'm cured? Go running back to my ex-husband who has a couple of new girlfriends, with their jaws set on straight, lavender scented armpits, and tight thighs with tight tendons that keeps everything on the bone? That ship has sailed for me, so I'm out to make the rusty boat I've got as pleasurable as possible.

And for a mort vivant, that centers around food, which means it centers around brains, and I really believe that my research can help others in my position.

Besides, I like the freedom of my day that I never had before. First Life was all about duties and responsibilities from cleaning house to going to work, to lint rolling my black pants to changing tires by the side of the road in the rain. Now, when I'm hungry, I eat. When I'm tired, I rest. When I feel like doing research, I do research. There's a real natural rhythm to it. And I don't miss my ex-husband all too much, or the green velour couch we bought at the thrift store, or the fresh squeezed orange juice we used to make on Sunday mornings while we did the crossword.

Or the baby we had, that I ate.

Her fontanelle hadn't even closed yet, so digging in to her skull was like peeling open a boiled peanut. I used to call her "my little peanut." That's so funny to me now that I used to call her that and then she opened right up like a boiled peanut. I know, this is shocking. Macabre. Something you'd read on the dark web. But before you judge, think a minute. You'd hear parents or grandparents say to babies, "I'm going to eat you up!" "Num, num, num," they'd say and pretend to eat their toes, savoring the ethanol of their stinky little feet, relishing the mouthfeel of their tiny appendages. It was born out of an abundance of love, love overflowing. How do I get more of this baby that I love? How do I ingest it, make it part of me? Perhaps even you have said this? So if I'm being honest, I don't mind that I ate the baby, even if it made my husband sad and I had to watch him from the window as he moped about with his shoulders sagging down and how everything seemed so exhausting to him, everything was an effort. He'd sigh when he got up from the velour couch, and he'd sigh when he came back with a fresh glass of wine and a brick of cheese and sat back down again.

Bob doesn't like it when he sees my ex's name as an incoming call on my cell phone. "Why doesn't he disconnect your number?" Bob asks. "Why do you still carry it around?"

He doesn't like it when I go by the old house either. He sees the way I look at my ex-husband through the window, and Bob is jealous. "I'll bet you wish I had hair like him," he says, rubbing his gray hand over his hairless and peeling skull.

"Hair just gets in the way," I say to appease him, but I know he knows.

"You can never eat his brains, Karin," he says to me. He looks small and desperate. "That's where I'd draw the line."

"I'd never do that to you," I say, and I mean it at the time.

Bob and I and the gang roam the streets, hunting. In the beginning, it was easy. It must have been what it felt like to the Native Americans when bison was plentiful. But nothing gold can stay, and the First Lifers are starting to run out, especially the smart ones.

I eat a lot of real estate agents these days, sort of mid-grade Olive Garden types of meals, but some of the zombies have figured it out, so a doctor or a chemist has become hard to come by. There's been a sharp decline in intellect in America to begin with. So few First Lifers read any more, so few extend themselves. So I hang out around the library and book shops, watching the delicacies come and go. I hang outside my ex-husband's house, and I think about his clever wit. I perseverate on how he could philosophize about the meanings of words, how his intelligence led him to overwhelming compassion for others. I swallow, wipe the drool from my mouth. But I made a promise to Bob, and I head home, belly growling and unsatisfied.

"I'm hungry," I tell Bob.

He shrugs. "What can I do?"

He's a helpless little man, and I feel sorry for him.

"Help me find food," I say. So Bob and I and the gang set out, and in a stroke of luck found a group of men dressed in jeans and t-shirts with video game logos. We cornered them and ate them. Turns out it was a cache of flat-earthers. Their brains were so flabby and full of gristle and tasted so coated with cheese dust that I almost gagged trying to choke them down.

One February evening during rounds, I felt my phone vibrate in the pocket of my cardigan. I knew it was my ex. It was always and only my ex. I ducked around the corner so Bob wouldn't see, and I read his text.

"I'm tired," the screen read. "So tired."

He included an emoji. The one with a frown and a single tear.

I used to know what it meant when my ex was sad. I used to know what to do. But now, all I could do was observe. I wanted to comfort him, but even this desire was a dim, echo of an emotion, and the impulses disappeared from my mind as soon as I thought them. My feet, though, kept on moving, pulled by an invisible force, to his house.

I saw through the window that he was holding a handgun. Where had he gotten a handgun? He was tossing it from hand to hand, feeling the weight. He looked in the mirror by the front door where I used to check my hair before heading out to Zumba class, and he raised the gun towards his reflection, his mouth saying words I couldn't hear through the pane of glass. He sat down on the couch and wrapped his lips around the barrel. He shook his head no, then put the gun to his temple.

A muscle in his forearm twitched.

The bang of the gun startled me, and when I brought my hands to my mouth as I would have done as a First Lifer, my pinkie finger fell to the ground with a wet thud. I pressed my face against the glass to get a better look. His body had slumped forward, and he was on his knees, his torso resting on the coffee table. He had a stemless wine glass filled with a thick red sitting on a coaster beside his mangled head. I had to chuckle.

I'd been trying to get him to use a coaster for years. I stared at the speckles of brain along the wall, along the green couch. They looked convenient, prepped bite size and still dripping with thoughts.

He was a member of Mensa, graduated top of his class, so I could make some assumptions, but I couldn't ever imagine the subtleties of taste. Would he be more sweet or salty? Would he be firm or tender? When I could wonder no longer, I pulled the key from its hiding place in the spider plant and entered through the back door. It smelled as it had during First Life, sandalwood candles, laundry soap, and slight mildew from the basement. I plucked a small tartrate of his brain off the wall, placed it in my mouth and squished it between my tongue and palate. Lush. Slightly burnt. Familiar. Like coming home for Thanksgiving turkey and cool pumpkin pie with his mother's home-made whipped cream. He tasted like birch, with hints of cherries. He tasted like him, brilliant and proud and under-appreciated, and I felt lonely, or the déjà vu once feeling lonely.

I went into the kitchen and snagged the ceramic bowl that we used for chips and pretzels and gathered all the bits of his brain. I plucked the sticky wads from the butter-colored wall, from the carpet we should have replaced last year, and I peeled chunks off the green velour couch until the bowl was full of him. I turned on the television, for which I had no remaining pleasure, but it was like habit, like instinct. News of wars and famine, drought and plague droned on while Second

Lifers ran amuck, and I ate my ex-husband's brains like a delicate, pan-seared foie gras.

# 3

# PROUD TO BE A SHRINER'S WIFE

Gretchen's been dating a 24-year-old professional boat racer from Brazil named Audato. She met him at the Kroger's, picking among the tomatoes and iceberg. Iceberg for Christ's sake. I could see if she were tiptoeing through the arugula or stroking suggestive spines of dragon fruit, but she met him shopping for the kind of bland, hot house salad my mother makes. Me? I'm the one eating the grapples, the cremini, the mesclun. If I weren't so proud to be a Shriner's wife, I'd wonder when *my* Brazilian would show.

Audato heads home in two weeks, and he's taking Gretchen with him. She's going to wait on the shore in a white pant suit and a blue scarf around her neck waving and smiling while he makes his way to the deck. I know this because I coached her out of the Macy's and into Gabrielle's downtown where she could get a properly made suit, and for more casual occasions, custom fitted jeans. The individualized tailoring only costs $50 more, and I wanted her to have them. She also tried on a stunning black bikini with little white dots and plump red cherries that laid out across her chest like a buffet. It lifted her breasts nicely, so nicely that it made Gretchen blush and hitch a minute or two before she agreed to let me buy it for her. We cut the tags and rolled the items neatly like cotton sushi and tucked them into two new, pink, hard-shelled luggage cases and set them beside her door three days before she was to leave.

When Audato came for Gretchen's goodbye dinner, he brought a pitcher of Brazilian sangria, which turned out to be an ecstatic blend of $6 wine, fruit punch, Sprite, and maraschino cherries. He'd actually brought two pitchers, one in a sweating glass pitcher, the other in a Tupperware container as a backup. We had a marvelous time, talking and laughing, listening to Audato wax poetic in his thick Portuguese accent. Gretchen stayed at his side, giggling girlishly, preening her hair, and popping breath mints after every round of drinks. The laughing exfoliated my soul, and even my dear husband, Petey, laughed so wide that I could see his row of silver fillings in the back of his mouth.

When we finished the last of the second pitcher, when most parties turn vulgar and sloppy, the evening continued to feel like it had healthful properties. Sure, Audato told slightly suggestive jokes, but they were about nuns, and that made it somehow OK because he was Catholic and, "you had to know religion to get them," he said.

This is how Baptists lose their religion, I thought, fuzzy headed and relaxed. One joke at a time. One dance at a time. One glass of Brazilian sangria at a time.

By midnight, I was drunk and no longer feared hell.

"I've converted to Catholicism," I said.

Petey put his hand on my thigh and stroked.

Audato raised his glass and said, "Mary bids you welcome."

"Don't welcome her too hard, Audato. She'll be Baptist again by morning," Petey said.

"Then I'll have to convert her all over again tomorrow night," Audato said.

"That'd be grand!" Petey said. "Why don't you come over tomorrow night around eight?"

I couldn't gauge Gretchen's response. Perhaps she wanted her last evening in the States to herself? But her body was non-committal with half her shoulder tucked behind Audato, her head turned towards him, so all I saw was her profile and the glint off of her new hooped earrings.

Audato clapped his hands together and said, "Tomorrow at eight."

Petey laid his head on my lap, rolled it back and forth a bit and then, finding a satisfied spot, fell asleep.

"I think he's out," I said, smoothing his eyebrows with my index finger, noticing that the skin around his eyes began to slide loosely over the bones.

When I looked up, Gretchen was fiddling with Audato's shoulder length hair and whispering into his ear, but he was looking directly at me in that hungry way that he has, his mouth partway open and his eyes fixed and focused.

He slid his tongue slightly between his teeth, and its pink tip poked through. A jolt of electricity fired between my legs.

I transferred my dear hubby's head from my lap to a pillow and walked to the kitchen with knobby kneed awkwardness caused by Audato's peculiar stare. I took one last glance in the living room before rounding the corner, and Gretchen, tipsy on Brazilian, was now kissing Audato's neck while he clutched her ribs, right where her bra strap would be if she had been wearing a bra.

I began clearing the counter tops, clanging the dishes loudly. I hoped that they would notice and excuse themselves before I had to yawn and ask, *Can I get you anything else*? A few moments later, they ambled into the kitchen proclaiming their goodbyes. Audato kissed me quickly on the lips, and a bit of his stubble scratched at my cheek. After the door clicked shut, I shut off the water, left the dishes to soak in the sink, and curled up on the couch with Petey. He looked so soft, so vulnerable in comparison to Audato. Petey worked in sales, so his skin was pale and smooth and soft. Even the whiskers of his 5 o'clock shadow were tender. I rubbed my cheek on his. He smiled in his sleep, pushed his pelvis toward me a few times, and settled back into a soft snore.

The next morning at breakfast, Petey had a headache from all the drinks, and he hunched over a bowl of oatmeal that was good for his cholesterol.

"That Audato is something," he said.

"Yup," I said, scraping a cold pat of butter over cold toast, black crumbs sticking to the pat.

"A real man's man."

"What does that *mean*, a real man's man?"

Audato had wide, proud shoulders and an open, confident walk. Masculinity, sexuality, and strength hovered about him. I would have agreed with "man's man," and I thought that term contained a bit of veiled jealousy, but I wanted to know exactly what men meant when they said it.

"Pleasure without intemperance, hospitality without rudeness, and jollity without coarseness."

He was quoting the Shriner's motto now, and I knew Audato had my husband's approval.

"I liked falling asleep listening to the sound of your voice," Petey said.

I set my butter knife down a little too clumsily, and it slid off the table and on to the floor.

"It was awkward for me," I said, bending down to pick it up.

"Mmmm," Petey said, but he didn't ask me what I'd meant.

There were no secrets between Petey and I, and if he would have asked, I would have told him. But he was reading the paper, and he'd had such a good time last night, and I didn't want to spoil it with speculation. I know which scabs to pick at and which ones to leave alone.

I moved to the living room and sat down on the couch to do some figures for Job's Daughters, the feminine order of the Shriner's, but it broke my concentration when I saw a pair of daddy long legs in the corner. I watched, thinking I might see a fight, but they stood side by side eyeballing one another. They cautiously approached one another, tapping the tips of their feet before planting them, small ticks at a time. They reached each other and the one spider, a little fairer in color, draped a shy leg over the other spider's leg, tentative and sweet. They eased toward each other, one leg at a time, until they were a spindly mat of legs and body. I swear I'd never seen anything quite so beautiful.

Petey came in the room, dragging his feet in slippers.

"What're you doing?" he said.

It was unlike me to be sitting still.

"Those spiders are making love," I said, surprised at the softness in my own voice.

I gestured toward the corner of the room with my coffee mug. Petey walked over to the copulating spiders, slid his glasses to the tip of his nose, and tilted his head up so that he could see them through bifocals.

Their round bodies were touching now, their legs lifting up and down, gently.

"Well, whattaya know?" he said too loudly.

His voice bellowed off the beige painted walls, and the spiders scattered.

My heart sunk. I felt sorry for them

"What'd you do that for?"

"Why'd I do what?"

Petey looked genuinely confused.

"You scared them," I said.

Petey laughed.

"Arachnid coitus interruptus," Petey said.

I couldn't think of anything to say, but since silence would have been misconstrued as brooding, I thought of the first thing that came to mind

"That's an awful lot of languages."

Petey cocked his head to the side and looked at me.

"Arachnid is Greek. Coitus interruptus is Latin," I said.

His fingers were tapping his jeans, a gesture he used when he was trying to figure something out.

Petey consulted a phone for a few minutes and said in a choppy attempt at Portuguese, "aracnideo coito interrompido."

It was a sad comparison to Audato's flowing, native tongue.

Petey and I had a good sex life, but it's because we worked at it. We kept communication open, spiced things up a little with some role playing, but nothing too crazy. I thought of Audato's long, sun-bleached hair and wondered for a brief second, maybe it wasn't even a second, if Petey was the kind of guy who would swing. Petey must have felt something funny about my thoughts because he opened his mouth to say something but closed it back up again. He slid his hand beneath the top buttons of his polo shirt and rubbed right along the line where his chest hairs formed.

Everything around me was getting sexy and restless. I saw it in Petey. In the brown, nubby bodies of the spiders. And Gretchen? She was happy. In love. But she also constantly picked at her hair, plumped her breasts in her new bras as if she were in a perpetual state of nervous grooming. God, and that new habit of compulsively chomping on breath mints.

When Petey and I had first made love 13 years ago, we laid around for days, languid, lazy, in an orgasm-induced stupidity. All we could muster the energy for was bottled water, a box of crackers and more sex. It's hard to not feel smug when you have a sex life like that.

But now here I was, my thighs anxiously bouncing up and down while I watched Daddy Long Leg porn. It was clearly time to get out of the house.

I made my way to the market, strolling through the produce aisles admiring the thick, fertile feel of an eggplant's purple skin as it gave way beneath my fingers. I smelled the sex life of flowers in the red, ripe strawberries. I intuited the stamen, the sepal, the powdery mystery of pollen. I gave over to the cliché and put the pint in my cart. I thought of Audato's tongue and bought a pink flower to tuck behind my ear. Its color would clash with Gretchen's red hair.

That night Audato brought Feijoada, a spicy black bean dish that my dear husband, a meat and potatoes man, loved. He sopped up the remaining juices with a piece of bread while Audato left his to crust and dry in the evening air. We drank maraschino liquor, courtesy of Audato, played a game of Spoons that Adauto had enjoyed in his childhood, and Audato this and Audato that. It was some version of The Audato Show, right down to his perfect hair and perfect smile and those trendy, retro, wide tabbed collars. And all of this was more than ok with me, with Petey, and with Gretchen who only took her eyes off Audato long enough to see how I was responding to him. When I winked my approval at her, she went right back to watching him.

We talked about his trek through the rainforests and how natural it was to enjoy a topless beach, and here's where *we* finally came into the conversation: Aren't Americans prudish with antiquated ideas about sex and the body?

"But it comes from our Puritan roots, so how can it be helped?" I wanted to know.

"We're all slaves to our culture," Audato said.

He rubbed his thumb behind the splice of unbuttoned collar.

"Unless we make the choice to be free," he said.

That look. That stare.

Petey had his pinkie finger in his ear, digging at an itch.

Gretchen sat there not slouching, not clicking her lips when she talked, not averting her eyes shyly while the rest of the party went on without her. I know it's odd to describe Gretchen by what she's not, but I realized I'd come to view her in void shape, the negative spaces. Here, under this Brazilian sun, Gretchen was developing substance.

"Would you like some more wine?" I asked.

"I don't like wine," she said.

"But you always drink wine," I insisted. "We had that marvelous red at Marie's."

"I don't like it," she said simply, without explanation, a bit of Portuguese hanging in her vowels.

Was this some sort of dig at me?

She stroked Audato's back and slid her hand down beneath his belt line, her fingers tickling his brown skin.

I fiddled with the flower tucked above my ear and said, "Remind me to give you that hair cream. I'm afraid of what that Brazilian sun will do to your highlights."

Gretchen ignored me and fingered Audato's sleeve. Audato cocked his head and raised a brow, a gesture that was an obvious invitation- but one that could also be denied if it wasn't met with an affirmative RSVP.

Petey, oblivious to anything subtle, jovially knocked back the rest of his drink and reached for the light saying, "It's getting dark."

I wondered for a brief moment how I could have married a man so obtuse. He relaxed back into the couch, and as the sun set, the light from my living room faded from a warm orange to a cool, purple hue. In the waning light, the lines and wrinkles of faces grew smooth and clean like plastic, and I wanted to live suspended in this space forever: the breeze coming in through the open window, the hum of the streetlights in the late summer heat, conversation about travel and art and things far away from my real life.

But the light faded quickly, and soon we were sitting in almost complete darkness. I heard the rustle of Audato's clothing as Gretchen rubbed his arm. I smelled her gardenia perfume when she laid her head in his lap. I imagined him stroking her hair, his fingers touching her lips. Petey put his feet in my lap. He tapped his socked feet together indicating that he wanted a foot rub. Instead, I cradled my glass of cherry liquor, the condensation rolling onto my fingers.

In the dark, all of my senses were heightened, and my heart had to work to accommodate the pain, the real pain, of experiencing life unfiltered in this way. It was a fantastic feeling, and Petey and I rode on the excitement of Audato and Gretchen's coming year. We even began to think about what exotic adventures might be available to us.

"We could meet you two in Rio," Petey said.

"Aaah, Rio is no good. Let's meet in Buzios. The water's like a baby's bath."

"Buzios it is," Petey said, his breath thick with sugary rum.

Like the rest of us, he'd had too many. He began to burrow his head into the pillow, and I knew that he was settling in to sleep.

"Oh no," I said. "You're staying awake tonight."

I squeezed his feet and twisted his toes.

"Ouch," Petey said.

"Come now, let the man sleep," Audato said in a way that shamed me.

And then Audato looked at me, square in the eyes, while he reached his hand inside of Gretchen's blouse. Gretchen raised her chest to meet his hand. Her eyes were closed, so I couldn't tell if she assumed no one could see because of the dark, but I sat there frozen and unblinking, not sure what to do.

"Petey," I said again, slapping his arm.

Audato retracted his hand and cooed, "Let's go for a walk in Petey's garden. Give Gretchen a goodbye tomato to remember you by."

He was already standing, Gretchen at his side, and I was desperate to be anywhere else but sitting in that living room, so we went out the back door, the porch light guiding our way a few yards until we ran out of patio and had to navigate by moonlight.

We tromped through the grass, the smell of summer ripe to the nose, sweet honeysuckle, fragrant tomato, a whiff of leaked oil from the garage intruding once or twice.

The locust's mating calls heaved and receded as we walked, Audato's voice and Gretchen's giggle cut through the hot, humid air.

I turned towards the tomato plants, thinking about how carefully Petey tended to the seeds, bathing them in fluorescent light, misting each delicate leaf before transferring them to the garden. He planted marigolds around the perimeter to keep intruders out, and when they matured, he propped their heavy vines on sturdy, white trellises. That morning, I'd seen a cluster of tomatoes so ripe, I knew all I'd have to do is touch the bottoms and they would fall, heavy, right into my palm with hardly any coaxing at all. I could still feel the sun's heat in their round bodies as I wrapped my hands around them. Then I felt Gretchen's fingers over mine, the both of us cradling the fruit. At the same time, Audato pushed against me from behind, dipped his head, and slid his nose up my neck.

"Oh," I said, trembling.

I looked at Gretchen for cues as to what to do.

But Gretchen was the opposite of trembling. Her body was firm, sturdy and solid, all of the ghost gone out of her. She kissed the back of Audato's neck as he took Petey's tomato from my hand and dropped it into the dirt to bruise. He kissed my wrist. When I didn't stop him, he nibbled up my arm until he settled on a tender spot inside of my elbow.

I wanted to call out to Petey, to shout his name and be rescued. I wanted to call to the mating spiders.

Audato's breath was on my neck. Gretchen's hand was on my thigh. Petey, God damn him, was asleep on the couch. Audato ran his teeth along my jaw line in small squeezes. Gretchen took my earlobe into her mouth, and soon Audato's mouth was on my mouth squeezing and sucking, the weight of his body pushing me down into the damp grass, the peppery scent of tomato plants being released into my hair.

It seems a simple thing to say. "Stop" or "No." One-syllable words, easy to get out, even if you've got shortened breath. But I couldn't make the sound or otherwise turn away, and my body pushed towards Audato's body. With one expert hand, he unbuttoned my jeans and was making his way towards the zipper when I heard the click of the backdoor unlatching, the whine of the screen door open.

Petey's voice cut through the dark. "Where'd every-one go?"

Where had I gone, I wondered.

Audato flexed his thighs, and in one smooth motion, he was standing.

"These are prize-winning," he said, his voice wet and slippery as he held up one of Petey's tomatoes.

Gretchen stood beside him, mute and smiling. Petey squinted into the dark. I wiped my mouth with the back of my hand, and Audato extended his hand to help me up.

Petey met us on the dewy grass and suggested a game of Canasta. But Audato and Gretchen, each carrying a ripe tomato, excused themselves and exited the party from the backyard, not backtracking their way through the house with its bright lighting and heavy domesticity. Petey wrapped his arms around my shoulders and escorted me up to the bedroom, whistling a samba.

# WHO'S A GOOD GIRL?

There are mountains in West Virginia that are wild and unclaimed, and my husband, Dante, sold all of his tech stocks and bought a plot of land on top of one of those mountains. A crew of men cleared a patch in his name, barely big enough to hide a house in between the trees, and I hadn't heard a word about it until it had a foundation and the wooden frames of 4 bedrooms, one for me and Dante, one for our boy, Ted, one for our girl, Meg, and one for all of our overnight guests. Before we had time to discuss it, the house had a kitchen with quartz countertops and an island with a second sink. It had two ovens, one for the turkey and the other for the sweet potato casserole and the green beans with French fried onions, enough to feed a crowd, and it never occurred to him that no one would drive those curved roads and ascend that mountain to visit.

To say that I was angry was an understatement, but I shouldn't have been surprised as his motto was, "It's better to beg forgiveness than it is to ask permission."

He paid his penance when I packed up the kids and moved back in with my widowed dad. The kids stayed in the refurbished basement rec room, and I slept in the bedroom I'd grown up in on the frilly canopy bed with cheap plastic finals, one of which fell off every time the door slammed shut too hard. The smell of my father's bratwurst and tobacco, coupled with his grumpy attitude, untampered by my mother's kindness and allowed to run wild after her death, drove me insane.

"Why is your hair like that?" he said to Ted, referring to the curls that fell below his earlobes, and Ted shrunk a little under his criticizing eye.

"You're getting chunky," he said to Meg, pinching her belly.

"Why doesn't your husband want you?" he asked me while the kids were lying on the floor watching TV with the sound low, hearing every word.

Even in these modern times, unless your husband is a known rake or quick with a fist, it's still mostly a woman's fault when a marriage falls apart. In my case, I was simultaneously too emasculating and too needy. After three weeks under siege at my dad's, I hit up a bar, ruining my 472 days of sobriety. It seems that I needed Dante to keep me square.

Dante made it easy for me to come home, putting on a pretense that he had caved to my demands, but the day after we moved back in, Dante drove me up the mountain to tour the new house.

"Just look at it," he said. "You'll see."

He had built my dream house and even improved upon it with solar panels and a real wood stove and a garden out back where I could grow beefsteak tomatoes and summer runners.

He showed me the well that dipped down into a spring so deep Dante said it would never run dry. He'd anticipated my argument to sulphur-smelling showers and installed a state-of-the-art water filtration system with alkaline, ionized water that was supposed to bolster good health.

"Like they have in Japan. 80-year-old women look 35 there," he said, appealing to my vanity.

I imagined filling a swimming pool with this ionized water and creating my own fountain of youth. I'd walk down the cement steps, healing my toes, my shins, the tender places between my legs, all the parts of me that felt dehydrated and stuffed in the back of a drawer.

Dante started the move without me and relocated mementoes from the house. Books, out of season clothes, a collection of DVD's we hadn't watched since digital streaming, and they disappeared like a shoreline slowly eroding. In their place, he brought a little yellow lab puppy outfitted in a big red bow. He held him up to his face and made his paw wave in my direction.

"We're not getting a dog," I said.

Meg called him "Happy" because his brown mouth was always smiling. I spent the next two months scrubbing puppy shit off of the rug.

We aimed to move after the kids got out of school in June. It was October 31st, and I had time to bow out if I had really wanted to, but finishing up a project at work and prepping for Halloween had stolen my attention. Ted went trick or treating as Homelander from *The Boys*, a show none of us had ever watched, and Meg went as Elsa from *Frozen 2* with a different costume than Elsa from *Frozen 1* that I had bought the previous year. Their outfits came from Target, and they looked cheap, the fabric so thin I could see Meg's jeans through the blue, nylon fabric. I was embarrassed for her walking around like that feeling like a princess when she looked so grotesquely proletariat.

My mother was a master seamstress and made artistic and convincing costumes for me every year. One year, Mom made me an authentic Native American costume with fringed leather and a genuine feather band across my forehead, but back then we called it "Indian," and "cultural appropriation" wasn't in our vocabulary.

"I feel so real," I'd said.

"That makes sense because you are real. We have some Susquehanna in us, and the extra bump on the molars to prove it."

I peered into her mouth with a flashlight to see them, but I counted only three bumps where there should have been four. When I told her this, she frowned, lit up a cigarette, and took a deep pull. She thought you could be anything you wanted if you wished for it hard enough.

I thought for a while that I could be a good writer. But I never thought I'd be good enough as a mother, and among the evidence were the short cuts I took all of the time. The piles of Lunchable lunches and hours letting them watch Nickelodeon formed a knot of guilt so big that I gave them each a $40 a week allowance.

Dante got into the tech industry at the height of the bubble when they were starving for even mediocre people. He slid right in to it, and as a point of pride, he never once slept in one of those pods or played ping pong or even drank the free energy drinks in the mini fridges. When I asked him why not, he always said he had work to do. Leave that to the kids who still need naps. But he used to joke at dinner parties that his job had a lenient work policy: he could work any 70 hours a week that he chose. So Dante left the house at 7 am and came home at 8 o'clock in the evening. I felt like a single mother, but no one felt the least bit sorry for me because the company gave out stocks like Skittles. We lived in a big house with a landscaper and a housekeeper, and because I never struggled with bills, none of it counted. Not the loneliness. Not all the hard work raising two kids by myself because getting a nanny was the line I could never cross.

I get it. I wouldn't feel bad for me either. Except sometimes I do.

The longer Dante worked in the tech industry, the more suspicious he got of technology in general, and he predicted that it would take over all our lives in the exact way that it did. That's why the kids were never allowed cell phones, why they never had a computer. He bought them an old Atari game that cost more than the Nintendo Switch, and even though they played for hours, Dante thought that this was better because the sheer scope of the new video games frightened him.

One day he got roped in to playing with his boss, and he paraglided so smoothly into *Legends of Zelda* that he bought the game for himself, then returned it, then bought it again. The plastic case sat unopened on his desk, the same way I kept an unopened handle of Vodka in the freezer. And this is where the idea of moving to the mountains was born in my husband's head. Why simulate the landscape when he could live happily ever after on a mountain of his own?

When he first approached me with the idea, he had already made up his mind. It was only a matter of setting me up to knock me down like a line of dominoes. As a salesman, he first stoked my longing, and then when that didn't work, my fears.

"Think of all the time we will spend together."

I'll admit, this touched a festering sore, a toothache with which I'd lived for the past 12 years.

He evoked one of my childhood fantasies when he brought home a signed, first edition of *Swiss Family Robinson*. I had to give him credit for remembering. We would give up Netflix and Hulu and our stupid smart phones, he told me. We'd do it before the kids would start to ask for one, and we would sit on our deck and look up at the stars. And when he took me up to check out the property, he had a picnic set up and a telescope with which to look into the night sky, and I was so lonely that I ached. If his love was water, I could have drunk an entire swimming pool of it.

"But what about my friends? What about my family? I'll go crazy up on that mountain alone," I said.

"But you won't be alone. You'll have us! You'll have me. We'll laze around in hammocks and read books. I'll read out loud to you," he chuckled. "I'll get rid of this phone once and for all."

I had always felt like I was a bore to him, and I could never get a foothold on his full attention. We'd play chess while he read the newspaper, we'd watch movies while he solved a crossword puzzle in ink. Once the four of us were in line at an amusement park waiting to get on The Little Dipper, and he was glued to work emails on his phone.

Standing beside him, I texted him. "Are you having fun?"

He looked up from his phone. We made eye contact. And he smiled.

When I had his attention, nothing could rattle me. But he went right back to his phone, and I felt like I had during my second week of sobriety and going through withdrawal. I had a Dante-specific hunger so deep in my body that it manifested as a physical pain, a deep ache below my breastbone.

Seeing my hesitancy with the new house, Dante tried a different tack, this time pressing his thumb on my fear.

"What kind of world is this for children, Arlene?"

Arlene. That was my mother's name. She was named after her mother, a strong and independent woman, a suffragette. I don't know how I'd come to be a tech salesman's wife. I felt so soft and weak in this role and an embarrassment to our family name.

"We can take them away from all of that," Dante said.

My boy was turning 11, and I set all of my fears into one compulsion. I didn't want him to see pornography. His golden hair was beginning to turn brown, and his little boy, outdoor smell started to turn funky. The thought of Teddy viewing bukkake made me sick.

My fears and the toll of remaining sober were turning to me to sawdust. I could ignite with a magnifying glass and a ray of sun. The last of my resistance was knocked down, and I succumbed to the dream that we'd have coffee on the deck in the mornings while the children slept in. In the evenings we'd sit on the porch and watch as they collected lightening bugs in jars. All of the holes and cracks would seal back up, and we would all become complete.

In the spring, we sold our house, took a big loss on it. We gave away our furniture and packed up the Ford F-150 with what Dante hadn't moved in or bought anew, and we left. Dante drove, I could never wield that hulk of a truck, and we watched out the back window and waved goodbye to the only house the children had known. We kept the windows down because the sun was hot for early spring, and Happy stuck his snout out the open window and panted excitedly.

On top of the mountain, Dante tinkered around, tying up loose ends. I planted a garden, the kids and I tended it, and I taught them what I had learned growing up with my grandparents in rural Appalachia. It's funny how it all came back to me, and my fingers remembered how deep to bury the seeds, when to water and when to withhold. And when the time came to harvest, we ate bitter cucumbers (the early 90-degree heat) but the tomatoes came up fine, and we ate those warm right off of the vine, having plenty left over to stuff into our pockets for canning later.

Happy became housebroken, and Meg taught him to sit and to shake and to stay. We kept him off leash, and he would run into the surrounding woods and come back smelling like pine needles. Once he came back with a large frog in his mouth, and in a panic, we all shouted, "Drop it!" Happy opened his soft muzzle, and the frog hopped away.

The kids did catch lightening bugs at dusk, and I often found the both of them sleeping in Ted's room inside a pillow fort, and though they never picked up *The Yellow Dog of Flanders* that Dante had staged in their bedrooms, they read *Harry Potter* to pass the time. Even Dante and I swayed in the hammock, and he read six books to me that summer. Six.

That season was tender. The days were long with nothing to do but tend the garden, polish the counter tops, wash the children's dirty feet. We carved a familiar trail through the woods behind our house, Happy going ahead of us by a few yards, stopping at every curve to make sure we were within eyesight. When I wanted a break from the kids or when Dante said something insensitive and bruising, I'd go out on the trail and sit on a big rock that looked out over the valley. Through the telescope Dante had bought for star gazing, I could spy on the houses down below, watch their clothes hanging on the lines to dry, count the abandoned pick-up trucks in the yard, and I could remember what life was like in the valley.

By the end of August, we had so much produce that I began canning the tomatoes, the beans, chopping and freezing the peppers. I baked loaves and loaves of zucchini bread that I romanticized eating by the fire in October with a cup of tea and thick smears of real butter, but I hesitated on picking the pumpkins because they were so small and feeble.

Then one day while the kids and I were playing Bocce out on the lawn, I felt a cool breeze brush over my shoulder. I shivered and looked out towards the east from where it came. A few trees had turned orange and were about to shake their leaves. Dante built a fire that night, and we gathered around it, still in our shorts and sleeveless summer tops, and toasted marshmallows over the flames. Dante mentioned ordering some snowshoes so we could still walk the trail, and after the children were in bed, I asked if we could take them to town to trick or treat, and I felt him out for a Thanksgiving trip to my dad's place. He was amenable to the idea, and I couldn't sleep all night because I was thinking about town and the people I loved off the mountain.

"Look at that," I said to Dante the next day as we lie in bed, my head cupped in his arm, his hand lazily stroking my shoulder.

I pointed to a stain on the ceiling above our bed. It was shaped like a fried egg with a yellow yoke and an oozing translucent white ring around it. It made me hungry for bacon. We'd eaten our entire stash in three weeks.

Dante jumped out of bed to inspect the damage, and I stuffed a pillow against my body where he had been.

"The roof is leaking," Dante said, his arms and torso long enough to pick at the chipping paint. "I'm going to check it out."

He was a joy to look at, especially with his arms outstretched in that way. His shoulders had turned tight and brown, his waist thinned out, and he appeared 10 years younger in a matter of months.

This made me curious about my own body, and I dug out the scale I'd hidden in the bathroom closet. I'd lost 15 pounds by tending the garden, going on infinite walks, and eating copious amounts of vegetables just to avoid canning them. Now that the scale told me so, I could feel a new kind of energy in the strength of my back, my core. I noticed that when I bent down to pick up a stray sock the kids had left around or to pull a burr in Happy's fur, I wasn't working around a layer of fat in the middle.

When the sun grew hot, Dante still hadn't come inside from repairing the roof, so I brought out a sandwich and some salted watermelon for lunch. When I didn't see him on the roof, I searched the perimeter of the house where I found him out back, digging a trench that moved away from the house towards the west.

"I brought you some grub," I said and held out the tray. A gust of wind blew hair into my face. I hadn't had it cut since spring, and it had grown long and wild, and since I never had anywhere to be, I'd taken to letting it dry natural and curly.

"Thank you. You can set it there," he motioned to his jacket on the ground.

"What are you doing?"

"I'm building an exhaust for the wood stove. I could see smoke coming from it, and I felt it would be best if no one saw that we were up here."

He wiped a bit of sweat with his thickly gloved hand.

"I'm going to route the chimney round the back side and over the next mountain."

He pointed west.

"So if someone sees it, they'll think it came from over there and pass us by."

"Your zombie apocalypse plan," I said and laughed. He looked so handsome in his jeans and his salt and pepper hair.

He smiled, and I realized then how little he actually did smile. This fact surprised me. I'd made up a Dante in my mind, and when I pictured him, he wore the same grin he'd sported on our first date, a trip to mini golf where we gobbled 99 cent pepperoni rolls and affirmed each other's dreams.

He scrambled out of the trench, wiped his hands on his jeans and eyed the tray.

"What'd you make?"

"Tomato sandwich," I said.

"I should have known," he said, laughing. "We're up to our ears in it."

He drained a bottle of that fancy Japanese water, and I watched his Adam's apple bob up and down.

He spread his flannel shirt on the ground and patted it to motion for me to sit. I did, and we talked about our favorite zombie show and how addicted to it we had been.

"It was all a waste of time," he said, but I wasn't so sure. Being scared made me cling to him.

When Dante had finished the last of his lunch, he brushed his hands, gave me a kiss, and said "Back to work."

He worked every day digging that trench and laying the chimney. He had it buried out through the lawn and had started moving in towards the woods where the ground was knotted with roots and stones, and the work went slower.

One night while massaging his tired shoulders, I asked him, "Can we get someone else to do that?"

"I don't want anyone up here that we don't know," he said.

"But we had work crews up here for months."

"Yeah, if I had to do that over again," he said, and his voice trailed off.

"Why can't you leave the pipe above ground?"

"Because then they could follow it."

"Who is "they"? I asked, but he didn't answer.

He kept right on digging and had miles and miles of potential woods to go. An infinity if he'd wanted it. I took the pint of Tito's out of the freezer, scraped a line of frost off with the nail of my middle finger before re-hiding it behind the peas.

After Labor Day, I took pics of the kids first day of "school" and we sat down at the kitchen table with our lesson plans and fresh books that still smelled like ink. I had a dream to give them a classical education, to teach them all of the histories and literature that I had never known. But they were used to the wild days of summer, and routine was difficult to develop. They complained about having to learn math, and the Shakespeare I was trying to teach them had no relevance to their lives. We worked at it for two hours before I became exhausted and let them out to play. They burst out the back-door shouting, "Wahoooo!"

They made up a running game with Happy and were at it for a long time before I saw them lying on their backs pointing up at the clouds. Happy lay between them, and Meg petted his fur absently. The leaves surrounding the house were a riot of reds, oranges, yellows. Because there was little rain, the leaves clung to the trees for weeks, and the sun burned warm in the cloudless sky.

Dante worked on the chimney, and when I wasn't arguing with the kids about school work, I chopped wood for the winter. Though we'd started stacking it when we moved in, there was still so much more to gather. I should have been put out by it, but the truth of it was, I liked handling the chainsaw, listening to its drone, deconstructing logs into hearth size pieces. It activated the same primal pull in my gut that made me enjoy chopping root vegetables for Hunter's Stew. We had the best of all worlds, living in luxury but in a way that satisfied that kernel of ourselves that was still hunter-gatherer. I had a good life and felt as if I had a cheat code to go instantly to the end of the game where the gold coins piled up like little mountains.

Soon the leaves dropped altogether, and everything turned gray. The sky, the bare tree limbs. The ground grew hard and brittle, and the wind bit through our coats like cold daggers. The kids spent most of their time indoors, picking at each other and making trails of messes all throughout the house. I couldn't keep up with nagging about it, and I couldn't keep up with cleaning it myself, so the detritus stayed, but the house was so big that it was easy to walk around and pretend that it didn't exist.

The floor to ceiling windows leeched heat, and the woodstove devoured more pine than I'd anticipated. I dressed in layers and wore my hat indoors, but I was the only one. The kids clothed themselves in sweatpants and t-shirts, and when I'd snag them for a quick hug at breakfast, they felt warm to the touch. Happy lay panting on the rug.

By this time, Dante was always outdoors. From the time the sun came up to the time it went down in the evenings.

"When do you think you'll be done with the chimney?" I asked one night in bed.

"I don't know. When I feel I've gone far enough."

The next morning, Happy vomited on the kitchen tile, and I cleaned it up with a paper towel and a splash of bleach. The kids groused about having oatmeal, so I let them eat the boxed cereal, even though we'd be out weeks before our next trip to town.

I slopped the oatmeal into Happy's bowl.

"Maybe this will settle your stomach."

He sniffed with his dry, brown nose and walked away.

I unloaded the dishwasher, scrubbed the oatmeal pot, sorted the Tupperware drawer, and then it was time for lunch. I made mac and cheese from a box for the kids, but I wasn't hungry. I'd lost my appetite, and food sat in my mouth like cotton. By now I'd lost 25 pounds, which I felt I should be proud of, but when I looked in the mirror, my bones appeared sharp, like sticks whittled in to weapons.

After lunch the kids whined at me.

"There's nothing to do."

"I'm bored."

"Build a puzzle," I said. "Write in your journal. Play a game."

My breath felt weighted down with dumbbells, and even speaking these words exhausted me.

They both whined even more.

"It's not my job to entertain you," I said. But I felt that it was my job. My miraculous mother had played endless rounds of Gin Rummy, Backgammon, and even Tag with me. The problem was that I was as bored as they were, and I didn't know any more than they did as to what to do about it.

"If you weren't here right now, you'd be in school. Is that what you want?"

"It'd be better than dying of boredom here," Meg said, and I supposed she was right.

"Dad's going to town in a few weeks. You wanna' go?"

I knew this would take some convincing, but the kids were already celebrating. Meg rushed to her room to pick an outfit.

As soon as I cleaned up lunch and threw in a load of laundry, it was time to make dinner. I pulled hamburger out of the freezer. From the other room I could hear the kids wrestling each other in a way that was about to turn unfriendly. Happy laid on his bed and whined. How many pounds of beef was I holding? The package felt unnaturally heavy. A can of stewed tomatoes took exactly 13 lumbering pumps of the hand-held opener. Even standing at the stove browning the meat felt like a marathon of shifting my weight from one hip to the other.

Happy let out a little growl, and I went to investigate. Faint smears of blood dotted the carpet and his overstuffed dog bed. I inspected his body. I gently lifted his paws, pressed on his belly. His ears felt hot to the touch. I dragged his bed over to the woodstove and patted it until Happy got in. Then I lay across his body, and he heated me from the bottom, and the woodstove warmed me from the top. I dozed off and dreamed I was in the city, seeing live music, watching plays, heading to work in heels with a briefcase in one hand and a latte in the other. I woke up to the sound of the fire alarm and a room full of smoke. I'd let the chili burn on the stove.

As I scrubbed the pot, the sun went down, and the house grew dark.

Dante came in through the garage door.

"What's that smell?"

"I burned dinner."

He flicked on the light, and I squinted.

"Why are you doing dishes in the dark?"

I shrugged.

"What's for dinner," he asked.

I shrugged again.

"We need to take Happy to the vet,"

"I can bump my trip up to next week," he said.

"I don't think he can wait until then."

He grabbed a pitcher of ionized water out of the fridge and poured it, iceless, into a glass.

What kind of person doesn't use ice? When did my husband become an ice-less man?

"What's for dinner?" he asked again.

"RUFF!" I barked.

This to me was a hilarious, hilarious joke, and I couldn't figure out why Dante wasn't laughing.

After dinner, Dante retreated to his office, and the kids played Atari in Ted's bedroom. I left the dishes on the table and joined Happy in front of the fire. I put my head on his chest and listened as his heartbeat played a sad and weak tune. I scratched him on the ear softly, told him he was a good boy. His tail twitched weakly. He was still smiling. His body moved up and down with his breath, so slow, so quiet. I could hear the air move down into his lungs, and I matched my breath with his. In and out. In and out. The pauses between breaths became a meditation in stillness as I tried to hold my breath. I stroked his golden fur and sat still as a stone, waiting.

5

# REBOUND

We had sex immediately in the club bathroom. We'd done it to break the ice, to get it out of the way. We'd done it pristinely, cleanly, in front of two mirrors, standing up because he said my abs looked better that way. We'd done it because I was newly single by 6 weeks and because I had sunk so low into a pool of loneliness that I was seeking a little comfort. I wanted a boost to my ego and to snap a selfie with someone who would make my ex-boyfriend jealous on social media. I placed one foot on the side of the sink as he grabbed my thigh and didn't complain when the paper towel dispenser bit into my back. His jawline was so chiseled and his dimples such a turn on that when the automatic toilet sensed our fucking and flushed, I pulled down my second orgasm.

We met on a swipe right kind of app, and this being my first meet-in-the-real-world match, I hadn't thought it through. While having sex him was great, I didn't consider what it would be like to stand next to a man this gorgeous and perfectly manicured. He'd been tweezed, moisturized, tailored, greased-up, de-fuzzed, de-odorized, and wholly de-humanized. Not only had he been clipped and waxed, his face appeared to be entirely de-follicled. He, like a photo in a magazine, had been airbrushed for $300 by the hippest salon, Fabo. He even chose an identity darker than his natural skin tone, and instead of Caucasian, he was a pleasing caramel brown. If he hadn't approached me first, I wouldn't have recognized him.

"It's Tru-Color©," he said by way of explanation.

"Ever heard of it? It's like a spray tan except with epoxy pore-fillers," he said as the bouncer scanned his phone to collect the $40 cover charge. "They'll last a good 6 hours without breaking down."

He didn't mind talking about it. Didn't seem to be embarrassed about it at all.

"Epoxy? That's safe to put into your openings like that?" I asked.

He flashed a perfectly white smile. "It looks great, right? Cinnamon Syrup, #492."

Some people are synthetically beautiful, and they are a product of the products they use. But Brendan came into this world with stunning looks. The orange, pink, and purple lights of the club changed with the pulse of the music and slid across his face and down the sides of his body. Each color highlighted a different part of his beauty. Red, his sculpted cheeks and long, straight nose. Blue, his clear skin.

"Yeah," I had to admit. "It does."

"And it's a natural antiperspirant."

I imagined him dipped and coated like a candy apple, the deliciously sweet shell holding little orbs of sweat inside.

There wasn't a single part of his body that I could isolate and say needed work. Beyond tight abs and broad shoulders, the man had his elbows bleached, and the pattern baldness on his shins had been transplanted with Nu-grow©.

And yet there was something unnerving about him, even the way he moved his perfect body on the dance floor. Everything was so smooth that it was difficult for me to look at him without feeling confused and a little bit dizzy. He was an impossible but wondrous M.C. Escher construction come to life. He was an equation where $2 + 2 = 5$. I could tell you in the moment that he was beautiful, but later, I couldn't describe any of his individual features. It's like his whole image was coated in Teflon, and my eyes slid right off of his body. Did he have shiny black hair and green eyes? Or curly brown hair and blue eyes? I couldn't remember seconds after looking at him, and I wondered if he'd register on celluloid film.

Standing next to a guy like that? There was so much… pressure. And my feeble efforts of colored contacts, false eyelashes, and more than my usual 23 ounces of liquid a day (in the form of lattes and energy drinks) couldn't hold a candle to his radiance. Even though we'd met at a venue with dim lighting, I couldn't compete with the way that the lines on his body blurred, or how his skin glowed right at the line of his muscle, highlighting his perfection.

This worry made the creases of my forehead gouge deeper, and the powder on my nose began to cake. My nose. It too was an equation that didn't add up, thin through the bridge but with a tumorous bulge at the end. Brendan kept looking at it, plucking at my insecurities with his stare.

"I can shade that for you," he said in a stupidly earnest tone.

I covered my nose with my hand and excused myself to apply a fresh coat of Curare®, but Brendan followed, I presumed, for another round of sex.

The trek was fraught with danger. To the left, a sea of women with perfect silhouettes. To the right, skin as clear and smooth as neoprene diving suits. The line from the bathroom snaked out from the hallway and women lined up against the wall of the dance floor, popping energy pills, reapplying lipstick. Brendan and I leaned against the wall, and I watched him scan the club with soft and dreamy eyes. We were in Generation Two of the Beauty Revolution and every person, man or woman, seemed to be made from the same basic stamp: large eyes, teeny, lizard-like noses. The two women in front of us in line looked so similar I would have thought they were clones except one was half a foot taller than the other. They both sported long, blonde hair extensions, the same Kohl eye liner, and most stunningly, the same matching pink, skin-tight body suits. Their nipples poked out so perfectly from the fabric that I wondered whether they were prosthetics or if they were sewn into the outfit. It didn't even occur to me that they might be real. But there was another, subtler difference between the two. The shorter one had a prettier nose, long and narrow with the most charming little upturn at the end as compared with her friend's porcine snout. Either of them could have snagged any guy or gal they wanted, including Brendan, and I watched him watching them, his pupils dilated to twice their size. The taller one felt his stare and turned to face him.

"Why, hello," she said, looking him up and down.

The shorter one followed her friend's eye line over her shoulder and turned. Getting an eyeful, she chimed in too, "Yes, hello there."

Brendan grinned and looked down at his shoes, a gesture so falsely diffident that I laughed out loud.

"This one's mine," the taller one said, drilling her eyes at Brendan's crotch as if I wasn't standing there with his arm thread through mine.

Her friend took a few steps forward and sunk her hip in a planted stance between them.

The threat of beautiful women coming to take my date rose in my body and warmed my cheeks. I wanted to tell the shorter one that she and her perfect nose could go fuck themselves. To let the both of them know that Brendan was my prize for the night. But even I didn't know why he was there with me instead of someone who looked like they did.

I wanted to tell them that they were too pretty to fight me, to fight each other. That looking this good made their lives easier, in case they didn't know. Brendan stood there, his eyes bouncing from one to the other as they bickered back and forth. Finally, the tension became so great that the taller woman balled her fingers into a fist and plowed it right into her friend's perfect nose. The force of the blow threw her body towards mine, and as a reflex, I grabbed hold of her hips, which had been padded to create a curvier shape. I tried pushing her forward, righting her torso for her to regain her balance, but her body weighed more than her tiny frame let on. I held her waist as we slumped to the floor, and she sat on my lap. The taller woman smirked and walked off.

Brendan kneeled at my side. A small wrinkle tried appearing between his brows, but they seemed to know they were no match for Botox, and they gave up almost instantly.

"Are you alright?" he asked.

Security weaved through the crowd, and in trying to get out of the way, I planted my palms on the club floor with the idea that I'd roll the body off of mine, but she was too heavy.

The woman began to stir.

"Are you ok?" I asked, marveling at how her hair had separated into perfect little ringlets.

"My nose!" she said and brought her hands to her face.

Two bouncers showed up. One looked as clean and smooth as a Hollywood actor, and the other like his stand-in who would never be put on film. He bent down so close to my face that I could feel the exhale of his breath on my cheek. He wasn't wearing any obvious make up, prosthetics, or filler, and he had a gap in between his two front teeth that he didn't hide with lips that were too tight. I had the urge to wiggle my tongue in between those parallel goal posts, and I bit my thumb nail to hold myself steady.

He wafted smelling salts beneath the woman's nose, and she lolled her head about dopily, avoiding the pungent stench. The bouncers lifted her to her feet and escorted her away as she hobbled in one high heeled shoe and one bare foot.

I rolled to my hands and knees to get up, but I felt a soft, squishy substance on the heel of my hand. Gum? A used condom? Jesus. Who tossed a used condom on the floor of a night club? I flicked my hand several times, but it would not budge. I held it up to the light, and a wet blob shimmered in the club's lights. I had no choice but to peel it off. As my finger dug into the wad, I began to realize what it was.

My heart trilled with excitement! I was a lucky bastard holding a real treasure: a technology so new, so innovative that it would transform beauty standards around the world.

This was like finding a Yartsa Gunbu mushroom on a casual hike.

Or a hunk of Jadeite on a group spelunking tour.

I had never wanted an object this much in all of my life, and here it was stuck to my palm: a Third Generation, Slimline, Instaplasty® nose.

The original owner was still in my eyeline, her curvaceous backside being escorted out of the club, and I could easily return the nose if I'd wanted to. These types of prosthetics are worth thousands of dollars, and if this had been a wallet, I wouldn't have debated turning it in. But this? This was different. This wasn't about money. This was a chance to change my life, update my ranking. Increase the number of guys like

Brendan I could score. I covered the nose with my free hand, hiding it from Brendan.

"Grab me some water?" I asked, trying not to crush the nose beneath my fingers. "Meet you at the bar?"

Once I was behind the locked bathroom door, I opened my palm to inspect the nose. I'd never seen one up close, and I held it up to light. I pressed at its vaguely elastic bridge. It was as cool and delicate as pudding skin. The flesh was, as the ads promised, real and living. Ironically, it even had pores that could be filled with epoxy. I gingerly rinsed it off in the sink, being extra careful not to tear the delicate tissues that laced the edges. Much like I'd lifted a dress to my body in front of a department store mirror picturing how it might fit, I lined up the nostril holes of the prosthetic to my own.

Someone pounded on the door.

"Just a minute," I said as the door handle jiggled.

I pressed the nose to my face and smoothed out the edges as gently as if I was handling wet paper. I looked in the mirror and nudged the flesh to the left, a little too hard so that the image staring back at me looked like a living Picasso. I course corrected to the right. There. The piece pinched my nostrils together and slimmed its line. It strengthened my face, gave me a look of confidence, maybe even intelligence? I looked at my reflection and blinked. It was me, but not me. 2+2=5. Somehow, my chin rose higher, the bags under my eyes receded.

The knocks on the door grew louder, more urgent. Music beat outside the door in an elevated pulse as if the entire club had taken amphetamines. I could feel its vibrations through my stilettos, another purchase I'd made after being newly single.

I unlocked the door and squared my shoulders, daring anyone to recognize the stolen nose or to sense that something wasn't quite right. But a trio of perfect girls in perfect plastic bodies didn't even glance my way as they spilled into the room and immediately swarmed the mirror. They pulled out travel-sized air brushes, breast plumpers, eyelash extenders, and got to work.

On my way back to Brendan, a man raised his drink in a cheerful gesture. A woman gave me a smile, soft and shy.

"Sorry I took so long," I said to Brendan, but he was busy at the bar, ordering drinks and flirting with the handsome bartender who looked very similar to himself.

"Hey there," he said to me, turning away from the bartender, but not before he shot him a quick wink.

"What do you think?" I asked, moving my hands around my face as if I was highlighting a prize package in a game show. I turned my head back and forth, looked at him out of the corner of my eye.

"Whoa, Baby, whatever you did, did the trick. You look great!"

"Wanna get a selfie?" I asked.

He raised a finger to his top lip.

"Some of that pheromone out of the vending machine?" he asked.

I shook my head.

"Fresh airbrush?"

I shook my head, felt the nose slip a little. I pressed at the bridge and the synthetic cilia knitted itself to my skin.

"It's my nose," I said.

I ran my finger down its length. Gave myself a boop.

"Oh my God. That's a limited edition Instaplasty®," he said, recognizing the brand immediately. "Those cost a fortune."

"Yeah, well, I found it," I said, and feeling sexy, widened my mouth and posed my tongue at the top of my upper lip. I'd never made that gesture before, but it felt appropriate given my new status as Girl with Pretty Nose.

His face contorted into a scowl. "That's someone else's Instoplasty®?"

"I rinsed it off first," I said.

He held my chin up to the light to appraise me. He nodded.

"Looks good," he said warming up to the idea.

He smiled, and I noticed that his teeth lined up at the gums, not just at the tooth level.

"Thanks," I said.

"What a world," he said.

"It was that girl's who was hitting on you."

He looked at me blankly. A million girls had probably hit on him since we'd arrived.

"The girl that got punched?" I said, letting my inflection rise into a question as I raised my phone, tilted my chin, and leaned into the camera lens. I clicked the button and checked the reel. Brendan looked fabulous, and the bulb at the end of my nose was brought to heel, but something wasn't quite right. I upped the beauty filter to 10.

"Your eyes were closed," I lied. "Let's take another one."

I put my cheek next to Brendan's and smiled. A faint polyurethane odor like a piece of freshly lacquered furniture oozed from his blocked pores. His hair smelled like varnish. I checked the new photo.

"That's a good one," Brendan said looking over my shoulder.

We stared at ourselves through the camera filter as we danced, Brendan's hands on my hips, grinding on me from behind. I felt an energy shift between us, like this could actually BE something.

Brendan spoke to the image on the screen that was me but not me, "You're something special," he said, and at the exact moment that he said it, I heard a small chipping sound emanating from his face, like a teeny tiny glass had broken. A red blotch appeared on his neck. Expiry time for the epoxy?

The sweet smell of male sweat reached my nostrils. Brendan's shell had cracked, and all his real secretions were leaking out. I lowered my phone and turned to face him. Something deep within me (in the pituitary gland? In the ovaries?) fired awake. My body felt alive and hungry, and I became desperate to get at the genuine maleness of his body. A whisker began to sprout on Brendan's cheek, and my amygdala, the reptilian part of my brain, lit up. In its humming, I licked a bead of sweat from his neck.

"Hey, hey now," Brendan said, wiping my saliva with a crisp, white handkerchief like some affective robber baron.

"C'mon, Brendan," I said pushing my body against his. "Loosen up."

I reached to tousle his hair, but the black strands crunched beneath my fingers. He grabbed hold of my wrist.

"Don't," he said.

His face was so new to me, and I tried to steady my gaze and memorize all of his features before they turned back into a blur.

"Let's do the camera thing," he said.

He reached out and grabbed my phone and began viewing me through the camera's filter.

I leaned in and around the phone and nipped at his perfectly pouty lip.

"Ouch," he said and put his hand to his mouth. "That's going to leave a mark."

The tiny part of Brendan's face that hadn't been frozen by beauty products squeezed into a tight knot of anger.

I tasted the iron tang of his blood on my tongue.

"Gimmie that," I said and snatched the phone. I held the camera up to him and viewed him through the filter, and then I turned it off. The images were identical.

I hit the selfie button and looked at myself. The person staring back at me was gorgeous, a perfect 10, but it reminded me of seitan trying to be bacon, and I felt like a fraud. Suddenly, I longed for wet secretions and musty smells. I had no patience for plasticine, no fortitude for fakery.

My blouse felt stiff and tight, so I unbuttoned it and let it slide off my shoulders.

"What are you doing?" Brendan asked.

"I'm skinny dipping," I said, "Swimming in a sea of plastic."

I unfastened the waist trainer that had been holding in my gut and took in my first deep breath in hours.

"People are starting to stare," Brendan said, widening the space between us.

I dropped the modern-day corset on the floor in front of me.

In the heat of the club, my eyelash glue began to give way, and I felt the heavy fringe hanging sideways on my eye like a loose tooth. It obstructed my vision, and I bumped into a girl holding a drink, and the liquid spilled on my dress. The tanned undercoat of my leg make-up began to run in thick ribbons down my thighs and calves giving the effect of melting wax. Cellulite revealed itself where my make-up had run. A stomach roll pushed over the elastic band of my panties like bread dough rising.

I paused then and looked Brendan in the eye.

I brought my hands to the Instaplasty® nose.

Brendan shook his head no.

I peeled the nose from my face and dangled it over the crowded dance floor.

"Don't do it," he said.

I opened my palm to release it, but the nose stuck there. I shook it a few times before it flung from my hand and attached itself, unnoticed, to the calf of a woman who was bent over, getting the most from her booty implants.

Brendan backed away from me as if I was someone he did not recognize, as if we hadn't had sex 45 minutes earlier. As if he hadn't said I was special.

The nose peeled itself from the woman's leg and fell to the floor in a small, wet tumble. As Brendan bent to pick it up, the woman shish ka bobbed it with her three-inch-high heel. It rose and fell, rose and fell with the music until finally, it dropped to the floor in several torn pieces of meat.

A bouncer grabbed me by both arms. It was the impeccably dressed partner of the smelling salts guy.

"You gotta' leave," he said pulling me toward the front door, his breath smelling like stale beer covered over by Listerine breath strips.

"What for?" I asked.

"You can't strip naked in here."

I pointed to a woman beside me wearing a bikini top and short shorts.

"What you mean is, 'you can't be ugly in here,' "I corrected.

I scanned the crowd, looking for Brendan. He was half-hidden in the crowd, shoulders drooping, his features sliding sadly off of his face. He looked at me sideways before he turned and disappeared into the sea of Vaseline-filtered bodies.

The bouncer ushered me into the night air. Outside of the club stood a string of flawless men and women reeking of silicone and chemical flowers waiting to be admitted past the velvet rope. Mixed among them were people who would never get in. They had skin tags, red marks, pores that dotted their arms, their legs, their backs that they naively tried to hide under a First-Generation beauty regime. The streetlights backlit and accentuated their sad, frizzy hair.

"You got a light?" a man asked behind me asked.

As I turned to look, I recognized him instantly. The perfectly imperfect bouncer.

I smiled widely, showing him my slightly askew incisor.

"I'll trade you for a smoke."

I searched my purse for the lighter I carried in case my eye liner needed warming, and as I looked, I tossed the various weaponry of beauty onto the pavement, the powdered foundation, the magnetized mascara, the tube of $300 CURARE® cream.

"That's quite an outfit you got there," he said.

I remembered that I'd tossed my shirt and waist trainer, that I was standing there in my bra and skirt, barefoot, holding my purse in one hand and my high heeled shoes in the other.

I was relieved to be in the presence of his soft, flawed, animal body, so when I saw a band of acne along his jawline, I ran my tongue over my teeth.

I found the lighter at the bottom of my bag.

"Aha!" I said and handed it to him.

He pulled a cigarette from the pack and put it between my teeth. He cupped his hands and flicked open the flame with his thumb to light me up first. The glow of the fire illuminated tiny rows of crow's feet in the corner of his eyes and those gap-toothed incisors that were a normal shade of eggshell. Best of all, there were those acne scars on his face, tiny little crags where my eyes could take hold. The tobacco ignited with a small yellow flame, and when I exhaled, the smoke billowed dragon-like from my flaring nostrils.

# 6

# THE EASY CHAIR

By Sunday afternoon, Fritz had completed construction on the tricked-out easy chair. He stood in his living room looking at it, his hand crooked in his chin, nodding. It was an odd contraption, a roller-coaster/ NASA launch-capsule hybrid covered in fake, blue velvet, with cushioned pistons and springs tacked on to it at odd angles. Not to mention the exposed wiring and that it took up at least 36 square feet in already small and crowded living room. But to Fritz, the machine was beautiful, a marvel of engineering if not of design. He sauntered around the perimeter, felt the sturdiness of the shoulder massager that lowered over the head, kicked at the foot apparatus as if it were a car tire. He left his pride and joy, only for a moment, to pour himself a rum and Diet Coke, the first one in a while. He took a sip of the old familiar and sighed. Relief was coming soon. And he had earned it. He was ready. Eager. But also a little nervous. He'd spent every spare minute of the last few weeks on this project, and it would break his heart if the thing didn't turn on or if it felt like any other massage chair.

He set the drink on the coffee table and began the process of entering the chair. He nestled his feet into the heated massaging pads and pulled the harness over his shoulders. He lined up the grooves in his spine with the grooves in the chair. He took a deep breath and flicked the activator button. The machine rocked to a supine position and began to hum.

He felt the vibrations in his thighs and in the middle of his back, about the 12th vertebra down. The chair heightened his senses and yes, Fritz knew it was the 12th vertebrae down. The chair shook loose some phlegm, and Fritz coughed. Too much force. He'd have to fix that.

He tried to exit the chair, but the thing would not turn off, and the straps above his head pinned him down. He pulled at the straps, but they did not budge. He tried slipping out sideways, but a bolt caught on his belt loop. The thing kicked at his kidney, and a jolt of pain sailed through his body. Even still, it dislodged a memory of his mother handing little Fritz a mug of steaming, hot coco topped high with marshmallow fluff, and Fritz's body relaxed.  It was both slightly painful and pleasantly sublime. Already, he hated the machine. Already, he loved the machine. The warmth of the coils began to spread the length of Fritz's body, and the hatred fell away until the only thing left was love.

Fritz poured a measured shot of rum into his glass then topped it off with a Diet Coke. The fizz felt good in his mouth; the slight burn on his throat made his shoulders relax. He finished this drink, made himself another and settled into his brown easy chair. Not the new one. This was the old chair, the harmless chair, the one without bite.

Fritz's jaw tensed, and the pinched nerve in his neck coiled, waiting for the drink to take effect. All Fritz wanted was to relax from the mundane pressures of the day, from his boss that always nagged at him, from his girlfriend, Tina, who required constant attention, from the minor aches and pains that started to appear at the back of his skull and at the side of his hip. Fritz's main vehicles for escape were sugary rum and outrageous daydreams, and he indulged in each freely and without guilt. When sober, he created in his mind lavish films featuring the beautiful redhead at his office who was not his boss nor his girlfriend. Wren was a skittish, delicate thing with the long, shapely legs of a movie star. Her large nose made her appear accessible amidst all that beauty, and he longed to dip his head to the side to get at her kiss.

Fritz had another drink and thought about telling his boss to screw off, that he wasn't going to re-do the goddamn reports. His mind filled in every possible detail: spittle collecting in the corners of Cragg's mouth, Cragg's stupid hard-soled shoes clicking angrily on the polished floor because he could not come up with a suitable retort.

And Wren? Wren would stand there impressed, breasts heaving, her pink tongue calling to him. Fritz would walk over and kiss her. She'd pull back slightly, but his strong right arm would hook around her waist and tug. He'd feel her exhale, feel her shrink beneath his hands.

Fritz's mind was bound by minute, exacting details like these that were hard to escape and had been hard to escape his whole life. There were benefits, he knew: He was an excellent engineer. His spice rack was alphabetized and easy to navigate. His girlfriend was more than satisfied in bed. But these never-stopping thoughts had their consequences.

Fritz clicked on the news without listening to it, downed his current drink in a hurry, then made another. Finally, Fritz's mind relaxed, and his daydreams grew gloriously blurry. Wren and his girlfriend tumbled in the same scene. He quit his job again, but this time he had no idea what he was wearing.

O bliss!

Fritz fell asleep, and his jaw grew slack, and a line of drool pooled at the corner of his mouth. If only it would last. But Fritz was roused 20 minutes later by a loud and brash infomercial, and when he righted his glasses that had fallen down his nose, he saw a timer in the corner of the screen counting down the minutes until the deal would expire. In his half asleep and drunken state, he took the timer personally, as if it was reminding him that his body was getting older, and he was wasting his time, goddamn it, working for a company that he hated, dating a girl that he didn't respect. Fritz maybe would have done something about his expiring body, his shitty boss, and his girlfriend who bored him, but these ideas were only peripheral in his mind because he employed the Sailor Jerry to keep them away.

Fritz wasn't entirely bombed, but he was too buzzed to find the remote, (it wasn't in the remote basket on his coffee table where he meticulously kept it) and his bones were too stiff to get up to find it. This is how they get you, Fritz thought, but he watched the infomercial with curiosity as a computer-generated image blasted red hot flames emanating from a skeleton's obviously hurting lumbar spine. Introduced to the scene was a beautifully upholstered self-massaging chair sporting brown leather, (also available in black leather and taupe corduroy) haloed in a brilliant white light. Fritz felt a twinge in his neck.

The skeleton grew flesh until it became a man, a man looking much like Fritz, tall, rather thinnish, but with more hair. The man pushed a button on the arm rest, and the red-hot flames turned to cooling waves. Fritz massaged his own red flames with his fingers and watched with guarded hopefulness. An animated cross section of the chair appeared on the screen, and Fritz saw that the secret of the chair was a row of hard-looking balls, like billiard balls, except these were vibrating as they descended the back.

A row of vibrating balls?

"Damn it!" Fritz said out loud to no one. "That's it? That isn't going to help anyone."

The next day at work, Fritz tested the pixels in the proposed infrared camera his company was soon to release to the public. For what use, he did not know, but he knew that commercials could make people want anything if it flicked at their desires in just the right way. He put his hand in front of the lens and saw that the tips of his fingers were completely black. White meant that the camera registered heat and warmth.

Black meant cold temperatures. Fritz wiggled his fingers and began to worry about his circulation. He thought about his hands turning blue and falling off. He thought about trying to re-attach them, wondered how he'd drive to the hospital with his wrists.

Focus, Fritz told himself. And like that, his mind obeyed. The pinched nerve in his neck and the subsequent numbness took a back seat, like one of those optical illusions: are you looking at a young woman with a feathered hat, or an old lady with a sagging jowl? Fritz could decide what in his mind was ground and which was focus, but unfortunately, this took up a lot of energy and could only really be achieved in limited increments during the day. Maybe 30 minutes here. An hour there. And the pain was ever present, which made it even more remarkable how gifted Fritz was at his work. He was meticulous and comprehensive, and he really did care, so the work came easy to him, and he completed all his tasks for each day before lunch.

So, he loitered on Facebook. He wrote his girlfriend an email, and when she popped on line 30 seconds later, they messaged for a good hour.

Tina: Hey baby

Fritz: Hey baby.

He had taken to mirroring her language and her body movements in order to subconsciously make her feel linked to him. He'd downloaded this gem from the website *How to Hypnotize Any Girl.* Sometimes it irked him that he was forced to use poor punctuation and capitalization when she messaged, but he had to ask himself: do you want to mirror Tina or not? To Fritz, life was one big trade off after another.

Tina: Whatcha doing?

Fritz: Testing pixels. What're you doing?

Tina: Thinking about you.

According to Tina's testimony, all she did was think of him. This annoyed him, but he had become addicted to it too. If she had for some reason decided to wane in her adoration, he wondered what else she had to offer him.  She didn't read. She was an awful cook. She wasn't even all that attractive. Her main good trait was that she loved him, and Fritz knew that for this reason alone, he was very, very lucky to have her.

Fritz: I mean at work. Aren't you doing any work?

Tina: I've got paychecks to post but they can wait.

There should be a comma before the coordinating conjunction, Fritz thought.

Tina worked at an impound lot and sat waiting until an unlucky customer came in to get their car out of hock. Fritz thought about how he could use that time. He'd read books, listen to podcasts, keep his mind sharp with Wordle. But Tina loved that she could smoke cigarettes at her desk and that she met interesting people. To hear her tell it, amazing people were streaming in all day long, and she had an infinite supply of stories to tell about them if the conversation between them had ever lulled. Fritz had picked her up from work one day, arriving his usual 20 minutes early (if you're not early, you're late, his mother had always said), but of the three unlucky people she'd helped that afternoon, he didn't find a single one of them the least bit fascinating.

Fritz: Mmmm.

Tina: I picked up a Stouffer's lasagna. Wanna come for dinner?

Fritz didn't want to go, but he didn't *not* want to go either.

Fritz: Sure.

Tina: 🙂 🙂 🙂

Fritz: 🙂 🙂 🙂

They talked like this for 50 more minutes, Tina doing all of the work of asking questions and listening to answers and thoughtfully commenting on each one before Fritz got tired of typing.

Fritz: I'd better get back to work.

Tina: ☹️

Fritz: ☹️ I know, Baby. I could talk to you all day but work calls.

He deliberated over whether "work calls" was an independent clause. If it was, then he needed to use a comma. Work is the subject. Calls is the verb. He backspaced to include a comma.

Tina: I know. I understand.

And she did. She was a wonderful woman in many ways.

Fritz logged off and surfed the Internet until it was time for lunch, shaking out his right hand every now and again, trying to bring it back to life as the nerves were constantly being pinched up stream where the shoulder met the arm. He checked his fingers with the infrared camera. Still black.

Wren came by Fritz's cubicle to remind him to turn in his time sheet. She barely looked up at him, and she acted like it was one big bother to do this reminding by sighing and relying on one hip to prop herself up.

"Can you have it by 5?" she asked.

Fritz saw how different she was from Tina. Yes, she was a brunette where Tina was a blonde. Wren was taller and thinner than Tina, and in physical appearance, Wren was a Yin to Tina's Yang. But it was more than that to him. Wren was cool to him. Indifferent. She had her own life outside of him, and Fritz felt a desire to insert himself into her world.

Fritz saw that Wren wore her hair differently today.

"Is that a new hairstyle?" Fritz asked while Wren was midstride, already on her way out.

"Yes, it is," she said, squeezing the end of a curl.

"You bring your lunch most days, don't you?"

He already knew the answer to this, but the hypnotism website taught him to create a "yes set." Ask two questions that you know will result in an affirmative, so the subject is primed to answer in an affirmative at the very next question.

"I do," she said.

This wasn't exactly a yes. He didn't know what the website said about this, but Fritz bravely pressed on.

"Would you like to go out for lunch today?" he said.

She stopped walking and fiddled with the opened manila file folder. Her tilted head told Fritz that she was unsure, so he nodded his head, slightly, almost imperceptibly, willing her to answer correctly. He did not know if it would work. He'd never had a chance to try it out on anyone other than Tina, and Wren was a sharp woman, and Fritz thought she might not be so easily persuaded.

"Why not?" Wren said, and Fritz leaned back in his chair, pleased.

Fritz decided on the quirky Indian Buffett that inexplicably included Greek cuisine too because it was some place new, and Fritz didn't want to take her any place that he had been with Tina. They piled their plates full of Mali Kofta, hummus, spanakopita, and Wren added a delicate pile of a la carte anchovies on the side of her plate. On their way back to their seats, Fritz felt someone staring from a table adjacent to the buffet, one of those invisible rods of attention that prickled the skin. He saw a blonde-haired man, someone he recognized but he could not remember from where. The man's eyes bored into him so intensely that Fritz nodded to break the tension, but the man continued staring, his eyebrows pinched.

Fritz put it out of his mind as he watched Wren sip a mango lassi. She left a small puff of fruity foam on her lip, and Fritz licked his own lips to soothe the ache that was growing within him.

"I did something foolish last night," Wren said.

Now there was a dot of red curry sauce sitting on the tip of that delicious nose of hers.

"You got a little something there," he said dabbing at his own nose in an attempt to embarrass her and thereby gain the upper hand.

This wasn't a game he liked to play, but *How to Hypnotize Any Woman* said to do this, and it wasn't Fritz's fault that the advice usually worked.

"Oh my. I'm a mess," Wren said looking down at her plate.

Now it was Fritz's chance to be magnanimous.

"It's OK. It happens to everyone," he said.

He could simultaneously make her feel bad and appease her fears. He was a one-man marketing team for the widget that was Fritz. She looked up at him, her nose still pointed towards the plate, her eyes big and open. And she smiled.

Over Wren's shoulder, he felt the blonde-man staring. He looked, and the man looked back with blue eyes. He knew those eyes from somewhere. Where was it? It wasn't from work. He knew that for sure. Was he the golf pro at the range? The guy at the drug store?

"You did something foolish?" asked Fritz.

"I ordered something from an infomercial."

"Please tell me that it wasn't the Kitchen Ninja," he said, wrinkling his nose.

"I wished that it was!" she said. There was a girlish giggle in her voice, and Fritz thought it so adorable, so charming that he wondered if there was a hypnotism website for women and if Wren was using its secrets on him.

"Well…" he prompted.

"It's a massage chair," she said and immediately covered her hands with her face.

A curl fell from her updo and pointed to her mouth like a question mark. Fritz felt a zap of electricity in his pubic bone, and he covered her hand with his, testing her reaction.

"I saw that infomercial last night. How about that?"

Wren wiggled her pinky finger beneath his hand. She raised her eyebrows. Fritz raised his.

"I was watching at the same time you were dialing."

They both laughed.

The man with the blonde hair stood up and tossed some dollar bills on the table. Fritz recognized that stance, that gait. The kind where someone who is short wants to make themselves taller so they walk, ever so slightly, on their tippy toes.

"I was thinking, though, that I could make a better chair than that."

"Oh yeah?" Wren said.

"Yeah. Definitely," he said. "All that chair is, is a vibrating mechanism with two balls traveling up and down at the spine. I'd do something more specific. Have a trap at the feet where it squeezes and releases compressions at specific pressure points and have a piece that lowers over the shoulders that actually rubs with nibs the size of thumbs so it felt like real human hands, and I'd include sensors so that it knows how hard to press. At the base of the spine, there should be more of a kneading action, and those hard balls? They're going to knot you up more than relax you. You've got to use something more organic to touch the body with. Neoprene maybe."

"Maybe you could make one of your own," Wren said, biting into a samosa. "After all, you are an engineer."

Fritz felt a sudden wave of embarrassment. Was she mocking him? He had been caught up, and instead of reflecting at the viewer what they already loved (themselves), he had revealed his real self, and he was not particularly pleased with his real self. He looked over at Wren to see if she had been put off. Her head was tilted downward looking at her plate, but the corners of her mouth were turned up into a smile, and he interpreted that she was enjoying herself. He examined the large bump on the bridge of her nose, and he began to get curious about her. What did she do in the evenings besides watch infomercials?

"What do you do in the evenings besides watch infomercials?"

He'd done it again and chided himself for following his natural curiosities.

"I love to knit," she said, and Fritz thought that absolutely pleasant.

"Maybe you can make me a scarf," he said.

It was June, and Fritz felt stupid for saying that.

"What? It's June," he said, putting up his arms and shrugging his shoulders. Raising his shoulders caused a sharp spasm at his collar bone.

"That's stupid," he said. "Make me a scarf in the springtime?"

He was stuttering all over himself.

Wren was smiling. Was she amused at his stupidity? His back pain began transforming into a migraine, seeping into the back of his left eye.

"Oh, it's the wisest thing you could've asked for," Wren said.  "Do you know how long it takes me to finish a project? If I start now, you might have it as a Christmas present."

She tucked her hair behind her ear. He smiled and smoothed out the rough of his beard. They each dipped a piece of pita into the same bowl of hummus.

They had so much fun talking at lunch, and they hadn't finished their discussion about favorite pizza toppings, so they agreed to meet on video chat that very night to continue.

"It's a date," Wren said, and just then the blonde-haired man approached their table.

"Fritz. It's good to see you again," he said but his face did not look at all like he was glad to see him. Instead, Fritz saw a subtle snarl on his lips as he looked from Fritz, to Wren, and back to Fritz again.

And then Fritz remembered. The blonde-haired man looked so familiar because he was Tina's twin brother. They had the same thin hair, the same squinting blue eyes, and the same short legs. They were as close as you'd expect fraternal twins to be, and Fritz heard a lot about him, but in the 4 years since he had been dating Tina, Fritz had only spent two afternoons with him, one watching a football game, and another at a wake when Tina's dad had died. Fritz preferred to have Tina all to himself, and so he usually did.

"Good to see you, Tom," he said.

All the while, Tom was staring at Wren as if she were a piece of gum stuck on his shoe.

"This is my co-worker, Wren," Fritz said, wondering if Tom had heard the word "date" and was afraid he was going to blab it to Tina as soon as he was out the door.

When he returned to work, Fritz checked email to see if there was anything from Tina. Instead, there was an email from his boss Craggs stating that he wanted the reports redone by Thursday. He was always redoing the reports for one stupid reason or another. Pain in his neck radiated past his shoulders, shot down his right arm and settled into his hand. Numb again. He rocked to the side in his so called "ergonomic" office chair, and this time the pain traveled down his spine, and spasmed once or twice below his shoulder blades before settling as a dull ache in his sacrum.

This was a daily occurrence now, and he had to do something. But what could he do? To distract himself, he thought about Wren's lips wrapped around that samosa, how flakes of phyllo grazed her lips before fluttering down the V neck of her white blouse, and landing, he imagined, on the crest of her cleavage. And what had she been saying? That he should design a chair of his own?

To focus, Fritz turned off his computer monitor, retrieved a tablet of graph paper and a special mechanical pencil he used when he wanted to be his most creative, and in 40 minutes drew up plans for a new, tricked out chair that he began to believe could really help his back. He imagined himself in the easy chair, pictured Wren ordering Indian take out from his couch. He put his hands behind his head in a confident gesture he had seen in a men's magazine, but the pain in his back wouldn't let him keep the pose. Just then, Craggs came by wearing one of his stupid, cheap ties.

"I need you to redo the reports," he said, looking past Fritz's shoulder and onto his desk.

"What for?" Fritz asked, putting the graph paper pad into a drawer.

"You included last month's data too," he said, frowning.

"That's what you asked me to do," Fritz said.

"Something wrong with your monitor?" Craggs asked.

"I don't think so," Fritz said, but before he could even finish, Craggs had reached over Fritz's shoulder and clicked the monitor's on button.

Messages from Tina appeared on the screen.

Tina: Tom said he saw you today.

Fritz's heart sank thinking of how he was going to have to talk his way around the situation, even though he didn't even DO anything. Fritz felt like he was always having to talk his way around things even when he was innocent.

"Looks like it's working fine," Craggs said, reading Fritz's personal messages. "Get those reports to me by tomorrow."

"By tomorrow," Fritz said, but instead, he messaged Tina.

Fritz: I was at a business lunch with a colleague.

Tina: Tom said she was very attractive.

Fritz: She has a big nose if you ask me.

Tina: Is she single?

Fritz's fingers hovered above the keys while he thought of a response.

Fritz: I don't know. That's not the kind of thing you talk about at a business lunch.

Tina: Tom said it looked like a personal lunch.

Fritz: I could try to set Tom up with her if that's what he wants.

Fritz felt clever for offering to arrange a date, but he also knew that he would not be doing this. Once he had calmed Tina down and promised her that he'd come by for dinner, he went online and bought compression devises from medical supply houses. He inquired on the phone about moleskin fabrics and temper-foam core that he could sew around harder, metal parts. By the end of the day, he had his plans in place and parts ordered.

When the clock on his laptop turned over to 5:00, he knew that he couldn't put off canceling his dinner with Tina any longer. Not if he wanted to meet up with Wren later that night.

Fritz: I'm not going to be able to make it.

Tina: Oh noooooo. Are you still full from Indian?

Fritz wondered how much Tom had told her.

Fritz: I knoooow. But I have reports to do.

Tina: I'll bring some pasta by the house.

Fritz: That's not necessary. I'll grab some quick take-out.

Tina was waiting in Fritz's driveway when he got home, so he had to park on the street.

"I brought lasagna," she said, kissing his cheek before he had a chance to get out of the car.

"But I got this," Fritz said, holding up a box of pizza, Wren's favorite: sausage and anchovies. He was going to try it while they video chatted, and she was tasting his favorite, ham and pineapple.

"I'm exhausted," Fritz said. "And my back is really bothering me."

Tina paused for a moment, and she opened her mouth. It looked like she was going to ask him something, something important, but instead all she said was, "Raincheck?"

"Raincheck," Fritz said.

They leaned in for a kiss, but they both stopped short, and the kiss hung in the air, undelivered.

When Fritz got inside, he set up his dining room table with plates, cutlery, and a candle. He checked his reflection in the downstairs bathroom mirror and video called Wren. They'd tasted each other's pies, called them delicious, and Fritz celebrated by making an anchovy swim through the air. Wren's tinkling laugh was still lingering in the air when Tina came bursting through the front door with her pedestrian "You hoo," and her hair up in a lazy bun he had just now noticed as a comparison to Wren's sleekly ironed bangs.

Tina was waving a stiff, pink bakery box. "I forgot your tiramisu."

Fritz closed the computer lid, but it was too late. Tina had heard Wren's song.

"Who's that?" she asked.

"Oh, it's a co-worker," he said. "We're working on this project."

"Is it the girl from lunch?" Tina asked, trying to sound non threated. Non-threatening. "I'd like to meet her."

Her chipped fingernails drummed on the now closed laptop. To her, this was a carefully chosen gesture made to appear casual. To Fritz it felt ominous.

"Oh, I'd like you to meet her," Fritz said, clearing his throat.

He didn't see any way around it and flipped open the lid of the laptop. Wren's long lashes and vibrant red lipstick, now beautifully glossed with pizza grease, filled the screen.

"Hi Wren," Tina said, waving to the camera. Noticing Wren's clear skin and perfectly lined up teeth, she added," I'm Tina, Fritz's girlfriend."

Wren kept on smiling, but her demeanor deflated a little, maybe so little that only Fritz had seen it. She put down her slice of pizza and dabbed her lips on a paper napkin.

Fritz said goodbye to Wren, accepted the dessert, and walked Tina out. She chatted as nonchalantly as when she had arrived, so Fritz relaxed a little, thinking that perhaps he had underestimated her. Once Tina's car drove out of view, Fritz tried to get back to his dinner with Wren, but she was gone. He waited, refreshing his screen every few minutes hoping to see the tell-tale green dot by her name. He saw Tina come on-line, and almost immediately a message came in inquiring about their relationship status. She didn't want to assume, but over the past 4 years she realized that she had assumed, and so she wanted to gain some clarity now. The knot in Fritz's neck began to buzz now, and the desire to fix his pain became more like a crusade.

Fritz spent the next three days avoiding his boss, messaging Tina as little as possible, and asking Wren questions. He spent the next three evenings drinking rum and Diet Cokes, relaxing in his old, subpar chair, and pouring over the new chair's blueprints. On Friday, when he got to work, he opened an email asking him to meet with HR about his job performance but pretended he hadn't read it. When he arrived home from work that day, boxes were sitting on his doorstep. Fritz stayed sober that night because he wanted to maintain his focus. He worked on the chair from Friday evening until Sunday morning. Sometimes he stopped to sleep or to grab a sandwich from the fridge, but still he stayed away from the rum. He'd been drinking too much of it lately anyway, and it made him feel superior to not drink it.

By the end of the week, the parts were roughly assembled, and Fritz had a mockup. Within a few weeks, Fritz gave it a test drive. The first test-drive didn't go so well. It attacked his kidneys, and he had gotten stuck in the chair and had to slide out beneath the straps. But he did have that sweet experience where the chair helped him conjure up that long-lost memory of his mother and her homemade cocoa. So he tinkered with the sensors, checked that the harness would lift.

Then he tucked his feet into the fleece-lined compartment and brought the device over his shoulders and strapped himself in. He hesitated for a moment before pressing the on button. He rubbed his back where his kidney had bruised and had second thoughts. He double-checked the wires, made sure that the newly installed emergency shut off button was lit. Once satisfied, he got back into the chair and rubbed his middle finger on the power button. Finally, Fritz pressed the switch, and the motors began to whir, and the chair came alive. The compressors compressed, the massagers massaged, and this movement, this motion on Fritz's body touched something in him. It was as if all the pain and longing stored in his tissues were knocked loose and released to run free in his body. An emotional pain formed at his breastbone and traveled north, perfectly north, and it caused his heart to tremble and his throat to knot. He thought about Tina. He thought about Wren. He thought about his Springer Spaniel, Harley, who had gotten run over by a car in third grade. Forty-five minutes later, exhausted, Fritz dozed off in the chair and slept a peaceful, dreamless sleep.

When he awoke on Monday morning, Fritz felt fuzzy and cotton headed. He made some coffee, raked a razor across his face, and put on a loosely knotted tie. On his way out the door, he tapped the chair and said, "See ya' later, Baby."

For all of his thoughts of the chair, Fritz could not concentrate on his work. He thought about the softness of the velvet, the radiant heat, the perfect way it squeezed at his muscles. Fritz was smitten.

Wren poked her head into his cubical.

"Knock, knock," she said, rapping on the top ridge of metal.

"Knock, knock," Fritz mirrored out of habit then shook his head and said, "Knock, knock? That makes no sense. I'm already in here."

"I think it's cute," said Wren.

Fritz ran his thumb over a Post-It notepad.

When he didn't speak, Wren filled in the gap, "Want to go to lunch?"

Throughout lunch, Fritz talked nonstop about the chair. When he returned to the office, he messaged Tina for an hour and a half about the chair.

Tina: I'll have to try it out

Fritz: Sure!

Fritz had said, "Sure!" but on the inside he was thinking about how he did not want to share the chair with anyone. Not even Wren. At 4:45 Fritz shut down his computer, packed up his things, and sat looking at the clock. By 5:01 he was in his car. He had forgotten all about his meeting with HR. His invention had stirred something in him that lasted beyond the time he was sitting in it. He decided to put on the rock and roll station instead of his usual classical music. Guitars wailed. Voices screamed. Fritz felt alive.

He strutted into the house and was going to hit the bathroom before sitting in the chair, but as he passed by, Fritz decided to sit in the chair for a minute first.

He sunk into the seat, jacket still on, and clicked the switch. Oh, oh, oh. Fritz closed his eyes and sunk even further in, ignoring the pressure building in his bladder. He allowed himself to be massaged and warmed for two good hours before he couldn't wait any longer. He reluctantly got up to go to the bathroom, grabbed a stale donut off the counter, and sat back in the chair.

He awoke twelve hours later with a half-eaten donut on his lap, feeling renewed and refreshed, but very, very hungry. He checked his messages, phone calls from Tina and from Wren, and ignoring them both, fixed himself an egg.

He put his dish in the sink and figured that before he got into the shower, he'd relax for one minute more. He sat. He put his feet into the snug compartment. The shoulder harness pressed tight against his skin. The chair closed up around him like a womb. He thought of his mother's chignon, his father's cologne. He thought about his high school girlfriend and the first time he had ever made love. The vibrations of the chair spoke to him, and Fritz listened.

He called off sick from work and ignored the repeated calls from first Craggs, then HR, and spent the entire, blissful day being caressed by his new machine. He daydreamed about the highlights of his life: playing high school football, joining the fraternity in college, the thrill of being on the cusp of twenty and all that was to come. A dark spot in his mind massaged the memory of his mother's funeral, then his father's death two months later. A deep sorrow spread through his bones, but the creeping black ooze felt good to him, like a massage gun aimed at all of his pain. This was an indulgence, not a curse, and all of the mixed feelings that swirled in his head about his parents, and all the things that Fritz could never admit, were pulled to the surface and allowed to breathe.

What relief.

When the day ended, he realized that he was hungry again, so the next day, after calling Craggs at 6 am with a message that he had the flu, set up a tray of food and water beside him. Berries. Cheeses. Pepperoni. Crackers and some Little Debbie snack cakes. There was no need to get out of the chair ever. Until he had to use the rest room again. He reluctantly got up, but being a clever man with attention to detail, he returned with a quart Tupperware pitcher, and he had no reason to get out of the chair the next day either. A full week went by and Fritz was still in the chair, detritus of used plates and crumpled napkins all around him.

On Wednesday, sores spread across the bottoms of Fritz's thighs, and a wet, open wound rubbed across the bony part of his sacrum. Fritz leaned to one side to relieve the pressure.

On Thursday, he was concentrating on the little nibbles the foot massager rubbed into his foot, when all of a sudden, Fritz felt a sharp, penetrating pain stab at the knuckle of his big toe, right foot. Fritz pulled his foot out of the boot and inspected it. Yes, blood soaked through the cotton on his socks and little groove marks were carved into the flesh. He reached inside the chair to investigate but found only smooth vinyl on top of foam padding. This struck Fritz as odd, but his desire for the chair overwhelmed his good sense, and he wriggled his toes back inside.

On Friday, the phone rang. Fritz ignored it and let it go to voice mail. It was HR telling him he had been terminated. His back spasmed. He brushed this aside as a threat. The phone rang again. It was Tina asking where he was, and this caused every muscle in his body to knot. Now he began to resent Tina because she was ruining his time in the chair. He closed his eyes and gave in to the soothing vibrations and heat. Every so often, a pain jabbed at his toe. Some were small nibbles, some were considerably more painful, but still Fritz felt the chair worth it. The phone rang again, and Fritz ignored it.

By Saturday, he had grown used to the pleasure-pain in his feet, and he was able to fall asleep easily. This time he had been dreaming of being a lion tamer in the circus. He had a top hat and a whip, and he had a lioness subdued and under his control. He had just put his head inside the lion's mouth when a blow to his shoulders jarred him out of sleep. One of the machine's roller balls had snapped back hard and had driven itself into the meat of his shoulder. He leaned forward and turned to inspect the device. After moving the parts carefully under his fingers, he could find nothing wrong with the wiring or the hardware.

Sunday night, Fritz forgot that he had been fired and called off work again for the entire next week. He hadn't taken a sick day in fourteen years. What could his boss say now except that he would be required to bring in a doctor's excuse? This worried Fritz, but he put the phone on the receiver and forgot all about it the minute he sunk back into the chair's velvet. All that day the phone rang and rang. Tina showed up at 5:30 PM with a small casserole of Hamburger Helper and a nervous smile.

"Where have you been?" Tina asked.

"I've been sick."

"What've you got? You know the flu's been going around."

Fritz was standing in the doorway but kept turning his head, eyeing the chair.

"Yeah, that's probably it. I feel terrible."

"Oh my gosh. You have bruises all over your neck! What happened?"

Fritz put his hand to his neck and lightly pushed. The skin beneath his fingers felt hot, and he became aware of the tender nature of the bruises. He looked in the mirror. His hair was unkempt, eyes were puffy and red, his teeth yellow, his mouth stringy with spit. Fritz was shocked by this, but what frightened him most was the wall of purple bruises that lay on his neck like a mottled sheet. He couldn't remember how he had gotten them or when.

"A side effect from the medicine probably," Fritz said. He didn't know why he said this. He wasn't on any medicine.

"What medicine?" Tina asked, her shoulders now at high alert, positioned at her ears.

For the first time in a long time, Fritz felt a pang of fear that he might lose her.

The two of them sat down at the table and ate the slightly warmed Hamburger Helper. The meal tasted delicious and salty to him, and he drank the cold beer she had brought in greedy guzzles. His muscles were weak, and he was tired, but it felt good to be sitting upright in a hard-backed chair talking with Tina. He had been in a dream state for days, feeling like an untethered balloon. Here, Tina gave him weight and an anchor. She asked him a series of questions that he could not answer.

"What have you been doing?"

"What have you been eating?"

"What does your doctor say?"

When he kept answering that he did not know she asked, "What have you been watching on tv?"

"Nothing. I haven't been watching anything."

He had been watching reruns of *I Love Lucy*, his mother's favorite show. That's all. He didn't know why he had lied about it.

"You haven't been watching anything? What have you been doing with yourself, you poor boy?"

She ran her fingers through his hair. Her hands cooled down his burning neck.

"I don't know, really." He shrugged.

"No?"

He gestured with his shoulder, "I've been sitting in my chair."

She followed his line of sight to the chair. Metal rods and wires poked out of it at odd angles. It had suffered some wear, but he hadn't realized how aesthetically unappealing the chair looked before now.

"Oh! That thing?" she raised her hand to her mouth in what looked like horror.

"Mmmmmmm."

Fritz was beginning to feel tired again, his leg muscles weak. Tina saw his shoulders sag.

"Maybe I'm judging it too harshly. Can I try it out?"

Fritz nodded. Though he felt protective of the chair, he saw no way around it but to help her get her feet into the correct position and lower the shoulder bar over her head. She smoothed out her hair, and Fritz flicked the switch.

"Oh!" Tina said.

Fritz saw her pleasure, and he wanted to get into the chair himself, but he had the strength to be polite, at least for a little while. He watched as Tina's muscles relaxed and her eyes closed, and he could see that in a matter of minutes, she was miles away from him. He sat on the couch and turned on the TV to wait. The voices droned on and on, but Fritz's eye was drawn to Tina's body. Pleasure had softened her features, and her mouth looked inviting to him. Her hips looked plush and supple. The chair's vibrations made her thighs and breasts jiggle in an appealing way. Fritz pulled down his pants and climbed on top of her. He pulled up her skirt, and she smiled, eyes still closed. She raised her hips so that he could slide down her panties. She opened her knees but kept her feet in the massager, her panties bunched at the ankles. The stretch in his back pulled at his tendons in a satisfying way, and Fritz could feel the vibrations come through Tina and onto his thighs.

When she had gone, Fritz had a deep desire to stretch out long on his bed--to lie face down, sideways, any way other than prone. Bed, with snapping clean sheets, called to him. He had a feeling that this was what was best for him physically and spiritually too. But even though the thought of sitting in the chair felt like a prison, he knew that it also felt good. There was something in the back of his mind about Wren that he wanted to remember. Maybe he loved her too? The chair could dislodge the emotions, bring it all into clear focus.

The phone rang. Fritz looked at it and tried to decide whether to answer it, but he took too long, and it went to voice mail.

"Hi, Fritz. This is Wren. I've made you some chicken noodle soup. I'd love to bring it by after work today."

Fritz looked at his phone. Fritz looked at the chair. He thought about Wren's fresh body, her beautiful heart. He thought he would test the chair out for a minute before he returned her call. He'd try it out and see. He climbed back into the chair, and it pulsed and vibrated a soothing lullaby. He fell asleep, Tina's face and Wren's face appeared before him, morphing into one.

He awoke to the harness snapping up and down on his shoulders, landing blow after blow into the tender strands of his trapezius. The chair pummeled him several times before it went after his feet, squeezing so hard that it caused a cramp in his arches. A hot pain seared in his eye as a rivet lacerated the cornea in his left eye, and his vision went out. Fritz felt like a boxer in a ring and blindly reached for the off button. He staggered out of the chair and inspected all the components but saw no reason for the malfunction. He tightened a few wires, greased a few joints, taped some gauze on his eye, and got back into the chair. The side of his face was in the process of swelling and turning purple. His entire body burned hot and tender. He moved his tongue around in his mouth, thick and dry. He smacked his lips and tasted blood. His tongue found a fleshy, open pocket, and Fritz realized that he was missing a tooth. He should get out of the chair. Fritz knew he should get out of the chair. But it was almost as if his body was moving without his consent. He slid his feet into the special compression compartment, lowered the chair's shoulder harness, and prepared himself for either pleasure or pain, no longer sure that he knew the difference between the two. From somewhere far away, he heard a knocking on the door. Or was it the sound of bird's wings, fluttering against a cage door?

# 7

# THE GIRL IN THE PIÑATA

When Walter heard the truck backing up into the driveway, he snuck to the window, opened a slice of the curtain, and peeked through the blinds, making sure that his trembling fingers weren't visible from the outside.

He felt faint with fear and chanted to himself, "Go away, go away, go away, please God, go away."

Instead, the unmarked delivery truck rolled past the driveway's edge and dug a deep, muddy groove in Walter's front lawn. A bead of sweat dripped from his temple.

The driver, an imposing man with a 5 o'clock shadow, jumped out of the cab, took one last drag of his cigarette and tossed the butt, still smoking, onto Walter's well-manicured lawn. Walter watched impotently through the blinds.

The doorbell rang. Walter held his breath but did not move. The bell rang again. Walter looked at where the cigarette fell. A dried leaf rolled close by. Did Walter see smoke rising from the grass? He shifted his weight.

Now the man pounded on the door, and Walter let his hands slide quietly from the blinds. He was not expecting anyone today. He stood motionless, pressed between the couch and the window trying not to breathe. He clenched then unclenched his hands. Finally, he heard the man's footsteps head back up the gravel driveway. Walter dared to peek out the window and saw, with gratitude, the man's sweaty back getting smaller and smaller.

Walter was desperate to get out to the yard to make sure that the cigarette butt was not lit, but something caught the truck driver's eye, and he bent down to inspect the lower left tire. He pushed at it with his hands. He kicked at it with his boot.

"Get into the truck, get into the truck, get into the truck," Walter said.

He often talked to himself because the cadence and the warmth of the vowels comforted him.

"Get into the truck," he said, this time drawing out the words, feeling their soothing vibrations in his throat. Did Walter see a yellow flame ignite in the grass?

The man walked to the rear of the truck and lifted the back door, and Walter watched as the man carried box after cardboard box to his front door. Walter hadn't ordered anything that required this many boxes, but this isn't what troubled him.

"The cigarette must surely be out now," Walter told himself. "It must surely be out."

As the truck emptied, the man disappeared deeper and deeper inside of it until at last he brought out an enormous, frilled, donkey piñata that was about four feet wide and six feet high. Wind blew through the rainbow-colored tissue paper, and to Walter it looked like a wet dog shuddering.

"That piñata's not going to fit," worried Walter, and sure enough, Walter watched as the delivery man leaned in with his shoulder, jammed the piñata onto Walter's covered porch, and its ears scraped the ceiling leaving red, scar-like lines on the grey paint. Satisfied, the man tucked a piece of paper into Walter's door, squeezed his shoulders around the donkey's haunches, and his boots banged down the steps, dropping clods of mud as he went.

As soon as the truck crested the hill, Walter opened the front door, pushed his way past the piñata, scrambled over the boxes, and rushed to the cigarette butt. He fell to his hands and knees and inspected it. Walter's shoulders relaxed. It had gone out.

He went back into the house, taking his shoes off at the door. He grabbed disposal supplies from the kitchen, put his shoes back on, picked up the butt with gloved hands and tucked it into a small Ziplock bag, making sure that the seal was tight. He took the bundle to his outside trash can where he untied one bag, inserted the Ziplock, and then retied the bag, placing the lid back on top, fastening the bungee cord to keep the raccoons out.

Next, Walter went about fluffing the grass where his knees had been, and he backed away, running his hands over where he had kneeled, making sure the lawn was smooth. Then, he went about inspecting the boxes. There were 32 in all. He examined the yellow carbon copy notice the delivery man had jammed into his screen door. "Paid in Full," it said.

Walter did not know what to do next, so he went inside to think. He got himself an iced tea and sat on the couch, but he could not keep still. He raised the venetian blinds half way, and the piñata's large eye stared back at him. Walter did not like having the blinds up. It made him feel exposed, but Walter wanted to keep an eye on the piñata, so he left the blinds where they were.

He rubbed the invoice between his fingers. He stared at the 800 number and memorized their digits. This brain work soothed him. For about five seconds, maybe six.

He paced the floor. He wiped the sweat from his neck with a cloth handkerchief. He opened his front door. The boxes were still there. Of course, they were still there. But Walter had hoped that somehow… by some miracle…

He picked up the phone, dialed 4 of the numbers. 1-800. His finger hovered above the next number, a 7.

"Just press the 7, Walter. You can do it."

The last part he said in his mother's encouraging voice.

If she were here, she would know what to do.

Walter pulled at his hair and hung up again. He inhaled, jumped a few times like a boxer about to launch into a ring, exhaled, and dialed the numbers again. He got all 11 of them pressed! But, when it began to ring, Walter thought about the voice on the end of the line, and he hung up again. The black eye peered at him through the window. Walter, exhausted, lowered the shade and went to bed.

The next morning, Walter prepared his oatmeal, his coffee, his half a glass of orange juice. He set the oatmeal in the middle of the placemat, put his coffee to the upper right, and aligned his orange juice in the middle above the plate where his mother always placed it "so that he wouldn't spill." Walter ate and sipped and looked at the yellow slip of paper sitting on the counter. He frowned as he cleaned up his dishes, washing them by hand, and setting them to dry on a hand towel spread out over top of his automatic dishwasher. He grinded his teeth as he wiped down the table.

He picked up the phone and dialed again. This time, he let it go through.

"Oriental Trading, How may I help you?" A woman's voice said.

Walter swallowed. He walked to the living room and looked out at the smiling piñata.

"Hello? How may I help you?"

Walter began to sweat. He hadn't talked to a live person in over three weeks. And even then, it was just to tell the delivery boy to keep the change.

"I got an order by mistake."

The wind outside kicked up. The donkey's paper fur swirled in a million directions. A piece of tissue covered the piñata's black eye, and it looked as if the creature had winked at Walter.

"Sir, you'll have to speak up. I can't hear you."

Walter repeated himself.

"I got an order by mistake."

"I'm sorry, Sir. I'm having a hard time hearing you. There was a mistake in your order?"

"No, I didn't order anything," he said.

There was a pause on the other end of the line.

"So you'd like to place an order then?"

Walter, near tears, said, "No, I don't want to order anything."

"Well, Sir, Can I answer a question about any of our products?"

"I don't have any questions."

The woman cleared her throat. Walter could hear her swallow.

"Well, what can I help you with today?"

Walter thought the woman sounded tired. Perturbed. He did not hear this kind of criticism coming from his mother, so when confronted with it, it made Walter very uncomfortable. But his mother was gone now. And this is the way the world was, and as she had said to him many times, "Walter, you will have to learn to make do."

"Well," he said, trying to make do.

"Yes?" she asked. "Please speak up, Sir."

Walter's heart pumped in his chest. His tongue thickened. He looked out the window and saw a squirrel chewing at the piñata's ear.

"Sir?"

The squirrel kicked up a cloud of shredded tissue paper, and it fell down around him like confetti.

"Sir?"

Walter hung up the phone and ran to the front door.

"Scat!" Walter said, but the squirrel was already bounding across the lawn with a tuft of the piñata's fur in its mouth.

The entire 2nd day went by without Walter calling about the packages on his doorstep. The squirrel had come and gone many times, and the poor donkey developed a bald spot, right in the same place as Walter, a small, perfect circle on the crown of his head. There was a light drizzle, too, and the boxes began to sag from the moisture. The sides of Walter's remaining hair began to frizz.

The next day Walter spent the time pacing the floor, holding the phone but not dialing, or alternately, dialing the phone and then hanging up. The sun came up and dried the moist cardboard until it became crisp. Walter's hair began to smooth. This gave Walter the confidence to try again. He looked this way at himself in the mirror, then that. He practiced his confident stare. He allowed himself to enjoy the straight, solid line of his nose, the bold cleft in his chin. He really was a good-looking man.

"That's order number Z2495495P?"

"Yes," Walter said, crisp and clear, perfectly enunciated.

He heard clicking and tapping of the computer on the other line.

"Yes, we do have that shipment as reported as lost in transit. We have already replaced that customer's order, and we would like you to keep the products shipped to you."

"But I don't want to purchase an oversized piñata," Walter said.

"You can keep the items free of charge," the woman said.

Walter's mustered vibrato was beginning to wane.

"But," he said.

"But."

"Sir, they are yours to keep free of charge. "

"But there are 32 boxes on my front step.  I don't want them."

But Walter said this last line so quietly, so meekly, that the woman did not hear.

"You're welcome, Sir.  Can I do anything else for you today?"

Walter did not have the gumption to repeat himself.

"Sir?"

Walter bit the skin on his lips. He thought of how long it would take to go through the boxes with gloved hands, sorting and bagging each piece. Just the thought of it paralyzed him, and he sat on the end of the phone line feeling small, so very small, and the piñata and boxes so very big. He didn't know how he could do it.

"Sir?"

Walter took in a breath to speak.

"Thank you for calling Oriental Trading. We value your business.  Please call again."

The empty line buzzed.

"I don't WANT your boxes!" he shouted.

He threw the phone across the room. It smashed against the wall, shattering the screen.

Walter began to feel unsanitary. He could feel grains of dirt beneath his fingertips, could smell the sweat that accumulated under his pits. A tidy pyramid of the last of his mother's home-made goat's milk soap sat on the green tiles of the bathroom countertop. He missed the goats. He missed his mother. He plucked a bar from the top of the pile and sniffed through the gray wrapper. The scent reminded him of her, a homey combination of oatmeal, vanilla, honey and just the smallest hint of cleansing lye. Wiry goat hairs stuck to the fabric of her work aprons, which were still hung up on hooks in her bedroom closet. He had kept his smaller bedroom, but sometimes he watched tv on her bed or took a soak in her tub.

He unwrapped the soap's package, first, the small jute bow. Then he ran his fingers down its seams, lifting the tape without tearing the paper. He smoothed the label and read: Mama Schmerdlap's Goat's Milk Soap. He cleaned himself in a healing mixture of water, lather, and the memories. Then, because he was thinking about the delivery on his porch, Walter did something that he never ever would have done before. He left the label, out of place, on the counter top and went outside to inspect the boxes.

The boxes felt brittle beneath Walter's fingers, and they smelled a little of mildew. He felt an empathy for the paper mâché beast because it displayed the wear and tear of travel and of storms, and Walter knew what that was like. But he felt a twinge of excitement too (was that the emotion? It had been so long) because who knows what could be inside?

The first box Walter opened contained party hats stacked into each other like nesting dolls- some were pointed at the ends, some fashioned like tiaras, some like top hats. Another box had several Pin the Tail on the Donkey sets, Mardi Gras beads, and a slew of laser pointers. With 31 more to go, Walter began to pick up the pace. There were Valentine plates, grass skirts for luaus, inflatable swimming pools and ball pits. Miles of red, pointed triangle banners were packaged in 6-yard increments. This was the detritus of 1,000 different theme parties, and they'd been shipwrecked on Walter's doorstep. What was he going to do with all of this stuff? He broke down the packaging, re-stacked the items, and found that they could be reduced to 9 boxes, which he labeled and stacked neatly in his finished basement.

The next morning, Walter sipped his coffee on the go and set the mug down, not on the placemat, but on the table's edge. He was eager to get the last of this business cleaned up, which meant the piñata, but the delivery man had shoved it so effectively onto his porch that Walter couldn't budge it forward or backward. He'd have to cut off the ears if he wanted to bring it inside. Walter went to the old goat barn to retrieve a hacksaw to do the job, and he found that it felt good to hear the sound of the latch opening and the barn door squeaking. He liked the way his boots felt on the soft, dirt floor. The tool was in its right place on the pegboard wall, and it was no time before Walter was able to free the donkey's ears.

Walter placed a towel beneath each paper mâché foot and slid the earless thing across the porch and in through the front door. The piñata was heavy with prizes that clicked happily every time he pushed against it. He pushed and pushed until he reached the empty wall that separated the living room from the dining room. It took up 1/4 of the living space and was shedding tissue paper like a Husky in August.

Now what? He didn't want to cut the creature. But still, Walter didn't want to venture out to deliver the piñata to someone else, so it sat there staring at Walter for three days. Walter would talk to it as he passed.

"How are you feeling today?"

And "My, it's windy outside. I'm glad we got you in here."

Being in the barn reminded him of his mother, so he opened her curio cabinet and began to explain her porcelain bell collection to the piñata. He selected one shaped like The Liberty Bell that commemorated the trip he'd taken with Mama when he was in 6th grade.

"That sounds pretty, doesn't it?" he said, shaking the bell.

"They all have a different tone. Sort of like snow-flakes."

The piñata stared at him. Walter looked at the top of his head where he had amputated his ears. Walter's skin pinkened.

"Oh, I'm so sorry, Pinny," Walter said, not realizing that he had named him.

Walter didn't enter the living room for five days. During that time, he thought about what treasures might be inside the paper donkey. Candy, of course. Perhaps some plastic whistles and some stickers? As the days went on, Walter began to fantasize that perhaps there were dollar bills inside, a stash of pirate gold, or maybe a woman? Walter pictured a blonde first, with pink, shiny lip gloss. Then a redhead with freckles like his own. Finally, Walter settled on a simple brunette with clean lines for her calves, knees, and hips.

Soon, the curiosity and the fantasy became too much for him, and Walter entered the room with the hacksaw behind his back.

"This will be better for you," Walter said. "The alternative is to die by beating."

Pinny stared bravely ahead and did not flinch.

As Walter began to saw at Pinny's neck, he soothed it with words like he'd done with the goats when he'd set them up to milk.

"It's gonna' be a hot one," Walter said.

The air kicked on and stirred the donkey's fur in a way that could have been construed as a nod. Walter wiped sweat from his forehead. As he sawed, bits of paper and dried glue floated about his immaculate living room. The head of the donkey fell downward, and an open hole appeared at the neck.

Walter peered in. No girl. No pirate gold. Just a mixture of chocolates and suckers and yoyos and paddleballs and stuffed animals and pins and pretend jewels and plastic necklaces and notebooks and any number of trinkets that Walter supposed children would enjoy, glinted at his flashlight's shine.

"True, there is no girl," he said, but Walter ran his hands through the loot, feeling rich.

The sheer abundance of it made Walter laugh out loud. He adorned his neck and his fingers with plastic jewels, tightened a foil wedding ring on his pinkie finger. He blew into a plastic kazoo. He inflated one red balloon, and the force of his breath made him dizzy. He picked out his favorite candies, settled himself on the couch and began mixing up the plastic tiles of a cheap puzzle. Walter wondered how his mother would have handled the piñata. He wondered if Pinny would have ever been invited into the house in the first place, and decided, No, his mother would have never allowed it. Walter felt a moment of proud independence, but then it dissolved into a loneliness so deep that it made Walter instantly sleepy. He curled his feet beneath himself and fell fast asleep in his jewelry and party ware without first sorting it and cleaning up.

On Sunday morning, Walter posted a sign at the top of his driveway that said, "Free candy for children!" On Sunday afternoon, the police showed up at his door. When they did not give up after three rings and instead began searching around the sides and back of the house, Walter answered the door. He showed the men the piñata. Showed the men the boxes stacked in the basement. He sent them out the door with two Ziplock bags full of plastic sheriff's badges that they could give to children. They were good natured and jolly, and when they left, Walter felt a tension in his mouth.   He brought his fingers to his lips and found that he had been smiling. He looked into the mirror-backed curio cabinet that housed his mother's bells to check his face. Walter's screwy grin looked back at him. He began to practice his smile. His lips parted too wide, and his teeth glinted white and wolf-like, and Walter frightened his own self.   He dialed back the intensity and settled on a serene upturn of the lips when his doorbell rang again.  Walter, presuming that it was the police again, answered immediately.

A small woman stood with the pad of her middle finger planted delicately on the doorbell button. She had clear white skin and large brown eyes with lashes so long they looked like wings, but what Walter noticed was her extraordinary set of hands. Her fingers were delicate and ethereal and brought to mind images of magic wands. Walter watched as the girl smoothed down her plaid dress, tucked her hair behind her ears.

"Free candy?" she inquired.

"Yes, yes, yes, right this way," he said. "Sorry for the mess. The mess.  The mess. "

The piñata was constantly molting, and a confetti of tissue paper lay scattered on the floor. Since he had made the sign that day and the cops had arrived, and now the woman, he hadn't had time to vacuum.

"Not at all," she said.

"Well, here it is," Walter said, gesturing with both hands towards Pinny. He became aware of his body, aware of his hands, aware of the way that his breath was shallow and how he couldn't catch it. He tried a smile, but it felt like a mask.

The woman peered into the neck, her head disappearing inside.

"Wow. That's a lot of candy."

"I know, I know, I know."

Walter watched her hand caress the edge of Pinny's neck.

"I call him Pinny," Walter said.

"Why hello, Pinny. It's a pleasure to make your acquaintance."

"My name is Chris Anne," she said, and her name echoed out of the piñata.

"Chrysanthemum?" Walter said, misunderstanding. "What a lovely, sunshiney name."

Her head appeared from the piñata with a brilliant smile. She did not correct him. Instead, she held up a handful of chocolates and asked, "Do you have a bag?"

He hadn't noticed before, but he could see now that she was a brunette. With clean lines.

"Yes, of course," he said and disappeared into the kitchen. When he returned, he had a cloth sack repurposed from the goat's feedbags. A little logo with his mother's image had been stamped on the front. He held it open, and Chrysanthemum dropped in the chocolates. She reached into the piñata a few times, and the two worked silently until the bag began to bulge. She reached in one more time and stood with her hands full, waiting for Walter to open the bag, when he said,

"You must really love chocolate."

Chrysanthemum blushed and let the contents of her full hands fall back into the piñata.

"They're for my students," she said apologetically.

"Of course," Walter said.

"Wouldn't they love some of these other doo dads? Hats? Puzzles? Balloons? Fake mustaches?"

"Just these will be fine," she said.

"You sure?" Walter asked, and he peeled the adhesive off of a mustache and pressed it to her lip. Her face felt soft and dewy, and this made Walter go soft too, and he felt a pleasant weakness run through his body.

She laughed and twirled her new mustache. Walter had never seen a woman so beautiful in real life.

"I'm sure," she said.

"Alright then, Chrysanthemum. It was lovely to meet you."

Chrysanthemum performed a sort of curtsy and smiled again and slung the bag over her back and headed out the front door.

"Come back if you'd like some more," he said.

"You mean it?" Chrysanthemum asked?

Walter nodded.

He watched her walk up the road, mustache still on, her flat ballet shoes clicking as they went.

Then, Walter waited for her to return. He waited on Monday. He waited on Tuesday. On Wednesday Walter wore his special derby hat. On Thursday he took it off. On Friday, he needed to go to the store, but instead, he waited. On Saturday he used powdered milk. On Sunday, he blew up a red balloon, but it only soared for a few seconds before bouncing sadly on the beige carpet and getting lodged beneath the coffee table.

But on Monday, Chrysanthemum came again!

He watched her fingers pick through the candies, sorting them. He watched her fingers push her hair behind her ears. He watched her fingers grow tight and clench as she talked about her sister who was a bully and never had anything kind to say to her. This last part made Walter sad to his bones, and a frown appeared on his face without any practice at all.

"But I've been doing all of the talking," Chrysanthemum said. "What about you?"

Walter began to perspire.

"What about me?"

"What is it that you do?" she asked. "You must do more than hand out free candy."

The truth of it was, Walter didn't do much of anything. Walter hadn't been out in many years, so he thought of things that he used to do when he did go out.

"I swim," he said.

Chrysanthemum nodded. "Me too."

She tipped her head upwards. He could tell that she was waiting to hear more.

"I hike," he said.

She smiled, and this encouraged him.

"And when I hike, I like to look at birds, and to press flowers."

He went to his mother's bookshelf and took down an old copy of Leaves of Grass. Within the pages were pressed pansies, violets, larkspur, rose petals and delphinium, tissue thin, delicate, and perfectly preserved. Walter could smell the chlorophyll, and it made him ache for his mother, made him ache for the sunshine, for the green grass, for the outdoors. The smell made him ache for love.

Chrysanthemum sighed, "They're lovely."

"We used to have a farm, and I used to make goat's milk soap."

"Oh!"

Her face beamed with pleasure.

"I'll get you some," he said.

He raced to the bathroom and plucked a bar of soap from the tiny pyramid he had stacked in the bathroom. Six bars left, but the thought of the dwindling stock didn't occur to Walter in this moment. She rubbed her beautiful fingers over the logo. She tugged at the jute string. She put the bar to her nose, closed her eyes, and sniffed.

"Thank you," she said quietly and tucked the soap into a pocket of her periwinkle skirt.

When she left that day, Walter called out, "Come back again."

Chrysanthemum laughed as she walked up the road. The sun was behind her, and he could see her legs in silhouette beneath her skirt. Dust kicked up at her ankles, dirtying her socks. Walter came inside, took off his shoes, went to the medicine cabinet, opened a bottle of Lexapro and swallowed two. He sat down on the couch to wait.

When Sunday came, Walter had on his best shirt. He had ventured out to the roadside to pick some Queen Anne's Lace and sat holding them, and when the doorbell rang, it had hardly stopped chiming before he had the door open and the flowers thrust towards the girl.

"For me?" she asked, blushing. "I should be bringing something for you."

Pinny's chocolate reserves were getting low, and Chrysanthemum was bent fully at the waist with her rump sticking out the top as she dug through the remains. He loved watching her do this, but it wasn't her thighs or her rounded bum as it bounced up and down that appealed to him. He loved watching Chrysanthemum's face appear and disappear like a game of peek a boo. Every time she popped out with her big smile, it was like a miniature surprise that a woman, a woman like her, was in his living room talking to her.

Finally, Walter took Pinny by the shoulders, dumped him upside down, and shook all of the contents out. They sat among the loot, sorting the goods. Walter stopped to watch her fingers move among the treasures. She worked slowly and seemed to never be in a hurry, so the sorting took a long, long time. Walter learned about Chrysanthemum's mother and how she swore she never talked at home and how everyone always got on her about it, but that Walter was such a good listener that she couldn't help herself.

"Well, you must talk a lot at school," Walter said. "You're probably tired by the end of the day. All of that instruction. All of those children."

Chrysanthemum frowned. "Yes," she said. "I'm tired by the end of the day."

She quit talking then and gathered her things and said, "It looks like we're to the end of the candy."

Walter's heart sank. He hadn't planned on ever running out of chocolate. Hadn't even thought about what it would be like if she didn't come back.

"I have more," he lied. "In the basement. Come back next week and we'll get it."

"I've taken plenty," she said, biting her lip.

"Oh, come now," he said. "It's for the children."

"Really. I've taken enough. You've been a wonderful friend to me, and I thank you. I'll miss coming by to see you."

"I'll miss you too," Walter said, and he sat down on the couch.

"We wouldn't have to miss each other," Chrysanthemum said, "if we didn't want to."

Chrysanthemum looked at Walter. Walter looked at Chrysanthemum.

"No, I suppose we wouldn't," Walter said, but neither of them knew what to do.

Neither of them knew what to say.

So, Chrysanthemum walked out the door, and Walter let her go. He stood at the door and watched her walk up the familiar hill. She reached inside the bag and ate a chocolate as she made the slow march uphill. Walter thought his heart was going split in two, but by now she was past the crest of the hill and this, this was too far from his home.

Walter went out his front door, walked to the end of the driveway and shouted out,

"Chrysanthemum! Chrysanthemum! Come Back!"

But she did not hear him.

Walter continued to take his pills. Walter continued walking out his front door and up his driveway. Every day he tried to take more and more steps forward toward Chrysanthemum. That's what his mother had told him. "Every day take one small step. You don't need to do it in big strides" and when she encouraged him, Walter could do anything. Walter had been swimming out on the lake. Walter had held a job as a security guard for the local college. But Walter had found himself stuck since his mother had been gone. He was tired of being alone, and he wanted to see Chrysanthemum again, so he walked to the crest of the hill, and he crept to where he had last seen her until he reached the curve in the road. He stood there, wanting to go farther, but where would she be? How would he find her? Every day Walter journeyed as far as he could. Every day he called out her name. Every day, when he got home, he talked to Pinny, who by now had his head and his ears reattached with duct tape.

"I still haven't found my friend," he said.

Pinny sat quietly, a good listener.

On Sunday, Walter was busy getting on his coat and his shoes for his daily walk when he heard the door bell ring. He walked quietly to the door and looked out of the peephole. It was Chrysanthemum. Seeing her made him want to leap, so he did just that. Walter leapt in place.  Walter smiled.  Walter opened the door, but when he did, he could see immediately that his piñata girl had been crying.

She stood there looking at him through puffy eyes with her arms crossed, her lip out.

"Do you want some more candy?" he asked.

Chrysanthemum shook her head no.

Walter said," I have some puzzles left."

Chrysanthemum shook her head again. Walter did not know what to do or what to say, so he fiddled with the door knob, pushing the lock in and out, in and out.

"Can I come in, please?" she said quietly.

"Yes, yes, yes," Walter said.

She did not take off her shoes, and small bits of dirt came off of the soles onto his beige carpet. Walter did not notice. Walter sat down at the other end of the couch, an entire cushion between them. Chrysanthemum began to cry.

"I'm not a school teacher," she said.

Walter didn't know the words that he was supposed to say, so he simply said what he thought.

"Who cares?"

She flopped her head into Walter's lap.

Walter stiffened.

"That's OK," Walter said.

"Aren't you angry that I've been lying to you?"

And Walter realized that he was not.

"I have a confession of my own," Walter said.

She rolled to her side, and the pink of her lipstick left a smear on Walter's trousers. He brought his hand awkwardly to her head and began to pat her brown hair. He felt her body shivering. Walter's pats turned into strokes. He pulled out individual curls of her hair and examined them.

"I haven't been swimming in a really long time, "Walter said.

"Don't worry about it," she said. "A person doesn't have to have recently done the back stroke to be a decent person."

Walter knew that she didn't understand, and as he was trying to figure out what to say, she spoke.

"I'm not a teacher," she said.

"A person doesn't have to have a class room to be a decent person," Walter said.

"I lied to you," she said and turned to face him.

Walter saw then how perfect her eyebrows were. Delicate little arches that he wanted to walk across to safety.

"I have a pig farm," she said. "They are my students. I have a small herd of Holstein pigs, and I've been taking the chocolate and making candy mash for them. I give it to them every Sunday as a special treat. They'll snort and get all excited when they know I'm coming. I have to tell them, "Now Daisy, She's the most aggressive, now Daisy, Settle down."

"You've been giving the chocolate to pigs?" Walter asked.

"Are you upset?" she asked.

Walter thought about this for a moment. He never spoke without thinking, so whatever came out of his mouth was the absolute truth as best as he could say it.

"No. Pigs are smarter than dogs you know, and I rather think that they might deserve a treat on Sundays just the same as everyone else."

Chrysanthemum sat up and wiped her eyes with the back of her hands.

"The police came to the house and said that we weren't zoned as a pig farm, and that I have a week to get rid of the pigs or they're coming after them, and I don't know what to do."

"Where do you live?" Walter asked quietly.

"On Piccadilly Drive," she said.

Piccadilly Drive lay parallel to Walter's place, and he could look out his backyard, down across the valley and see her street winding behind his. All along there had been a short cut just through the fields and a few brambles, and one small creek that was usually dry except in the spring time.

"Let's go look," Walter said, and guided her to his back porch and gestured to her road.

"Which one is your home," he asked but he already knew. He had often watched the pigs in their pen, just little dots from that far away.

She pointed towards the small, red-roofed house a little to the right. Her property and his joined at a corner.

"Why didn't you come through the valley to get the candy?" Walter asked. "Why go all the way around?"

He could see the small pen where her pigs were milling about. He imagined her approaching the pen with the candy mash made from his piñata. He imagined them gathering around her pretty calves, grunting and snorting at her ankles.

"Because that's private property. I didn't want to go stomping around where I hadn't been invited."

That was something Walter himself would have said.

"I needed to be invited, and besides, sometimes you just can't take the shortcut."

This also was something Walter would have said.

Chrysanthemum looked up at him. Her eyes were large and brown, her lips pushed out, receptive to Walter, and even Walter who did not know women at all, could see yearning. Walter leaned in and kissed her on the lips, and it felt to him as if he had just let go of the string of a balloon, and tied to that balloon was his heart, and it soared into the air. It went high above the trees and beyond the valley, and caught by the wind, it traveled anywhere that it wanted to go and nothing would ever tell it to come down.

When they parted, Walter stared at her hair as it curled just at her shoulders. He looked at her cardigan, at her dress and the bruises on her calves and her scraped up ankles and the scuffed tennis shoes below them. He remembered his mother's own bruises from tending the goats.

Walter said quietly, "Come with me," and he led Chrysanthemum to his mother's bedroom. He pulled one of his mother's farming aprons off of its peg and placed it around her neck. He placed one around his own neck too. He went to the basement and gathered the garland, the string of flags, the wrapping ribbon and party hats. Walter led her to the empty goat pens, and he pushed on the fences.

"Sturdy," he said. "Still sturdy."

He inspected a small hole in the fence that would need mending within the week, but all in all, things looked solid.

"They can stay here," he said.

"I couldn't," Chrysanthemum said.

"Why not?" Walter asked.

"I don't want to take advantage," she said.

"It's serendipity," he said, and it felt so good to him to give.

"C'mon. We've got work to do. Pigs are hard to herd but not impossible."

He tied a length of silver tinsel garland to a pole of the goat pen's gate and instructed Chrysanthemum to move further down a yard or two and hold the line tight and steady while he secured the garland with a stick so that it formed a make shift fence. Walter and Chrysanthemum began to weave a party favor path from the empty goat pen down the valley towards Chrysanthemum's pigs. When they ran out of tinsel, they used flags, and when they ran out of flags, they used banners.

As they worked, Walter moved farther and farther away from his home. At times panic moved in his heart, but then he would hold steady to the line tied on one end to his mother's goat pen and when he needed extra strength, he looked farther down the valley at Chrysanthemum as she pulled the line ahead of him, paving the way, and Walter's balloon heart floated out past the county line.

# 8

# LIMBO PARTY AT THE DIG SITE

I don't know whose idea it was to light the limbo stick on fire, but I was totally down for it. We all were. Our little team of archaeology students had excavated surfer movies from the 60's, and we wanted to live like these movie stars but also do it on an intern's budget. Give us a stick, a little accelerant, a record player, and the tool shed with the trowels and brushes and khaki hats pushed toward the wall, and it's all we needed to create a little late-teen, early adulthood danger. We propped up the game, and Manny, who spent a summer in Trinidad, said that they lit the sticks on fire with rum. We were young, and in a hurry, and didn't want to waste our booze, so we used gasoline instead.

Fear was scarce then because bad things happened to other people, and without the internet to tell us not to, we cooked with bacon grease that sat on our stoves for months, left the chords of our blinds sway about like little nooses, and we danced Limbo underneath a gasoline fire.

It was Lou who doused the stick and Manny and Kent who propped it up, and once it was alit, Lou set the needle down on top of the record, and Calypso spun out of the crackling, built-in speakers. Little bits of fire dripped off the pole onto the concrete floor of the shed, and Barbara, a tall brunette and a sophomore, was the first to go. She leaned back, letting her long, brown hair fan out upon the ground as she worked her thighs, moving that body in slow inches. The yellow of the fire glowed across bottom of her jawline, reminding me of the time I played the buttercup game with the neighbor boy, Doug Bailey, who may have been the first boy I ever loved.

The rules said to hold the yellow flower beneath your beloved's chin. If the buttercup reflected its sunshine on the skin, it meant that the person loved you. If there was no reflection of yellow, they did not. It was such simple technology, and we sat on the grass Indian style, knees touching, and Doug and I blinked in slow motion and felt every tick of the clock as he held the flower to my chin. Were we to kiss? Were we to part as friends?

An ant crawled from my body to his, and the tickle of its feet was a curiosity, and we watched it walk on its tiny little legs over our scabbed knees.

And all of this waiting was OK because we had nowhere else to go but where we were at the time. Nowadays you have to re-learn how to be in the present moment with a meditation app sponsored by Juul vape pens.

My parents had done such a great job raising me that when Doug told me that the flower came up empty, I didn't believe him. I knew he was lying because he had to like me, and denying it was just how boys were. They didn't tell you their feelings except by punching your arm or grabbing your rear. You can't do those things nowadays, but while the breezes were blowing and ants were crawling, this kind of flirting was a way to pass time.

But things speed up when you are eighteen and on an archaeological dig and you're too impatient to use a brush instead of a pickaxe and you get to feeling that something isn't right with you. Your feet wander too much, and you can't sit still, and you wonder if this kind of pain will ever leave you.

Being teenagers, we rushed everything ahead. We were too young to legally drink, but we drank. We were too young to understand politics, but we were activists at campus rallies. We rushed sex too and dug our noses deep into the crotches of the opposite sex, and in some cases the same sex, and we straddled our partners like we'd seen in magazines and like some of us had seen in darkened movie houses before there was the internet.

Porn's impossible to avoid if you have a single curious hair, and kids see it all in video and even in 3D virtual reality with a hacked head set before they can get to the real thing. And that kind of whitewashes it, and it's all so fake anyhow. Lighting here, moan-track there, women coming into thin air with no direct stimulation to the clit. What's this teach a boy about a woman's body? What's this teach a woman about her own body?

Back then, bodies were raw and genuine. They were full of hair and secret places for scent to stick, and balls smelled like balls, and pussies still smelled earthy and thick, like ozone after a lightning storm. You used to be able to walk into a roommate's living room and smell sex in the air and get that little trill in your pubic bone, knowing what they'd been up to, but those days are gone. Now everything smells like candles and body wax and pumpkin flavored lube. Where's the honesty? It's a shame really. Kids today don't know what they're missing.

And kids today would never go near a burning limbo stick, dripping flames. Maybe it's because they know better, but it sure as heck isn't because they're living better.

We were alive in those days, and we were playing in a hurry, rushing our turn as another section of the pole burned off from the stick and caught on the tip of Barb's bangs. As she stood up, the small flame extinguished itself, but the shed filled with the gloomy singe of burnt hair.

Kent was up next. He had strong torso muscles, not like they do today with every single ab bulging out to where you can count them, and it's all too much, but Kent was a handsome guy. He was a fit guy for back in the day, at a time when everyone was thin, and he had no trouble clearing the pole. And then Manny. And then Lou. And then it was my turn.

I wanted to do it. I was eager to do it. I had confidence in the command of my body, and I thought that in the same way that Doug Bailey must love me, the fire must love me too. And I leaned back, became acutely aware of the tension in my thighs, my buttocks. I felt the curvature of my spine.

The heat began at my navel and crawled up my breast and burned hot on the top of my chin that Doug had tilted and brushed with that petal. Once I cleared the bar, I unfolded each vertebra, not rushing, not hurrying, thinking of Doug's brown eyes and willing time to slow down. But time is inevitable, and once I stood, the world began moving again.

Manny put a rum and Coke in my palm and tipped the bottom of the glass until I had drained it. He put his dark hands on my hip bones, and I loved the brown of his fingers and how they looked next to the white of my skin, and I was back to wanting to burn time until later when Manny and I would go back up to the dig and sit in the dark and we would talk for a few polite minutes before we began rushing our bodies ahead of our hearts and fingers started picking their way through clothes, exploring folds and dark places like hungry boll weevils devouring all of the cotton clothing in its path.

The fire was starting to really crackle now, and every snap made us jump. Barbara was smiling tightly and smoothing down her dress. Lou was watching her move. We each did another round. A hot cinder floated down onto Lou's thigh and burned a hole in his shorts, and we lowered the flaming stick another few inches. Barbara practiced yoga, very new and trendy in the U.S. at the time, and her nimble body defied gravity as her back lie parallel to the flames. Lou tried, but he is rounder than the rest and fell onto his back, so Manny dragged him away from the flames by his ankles.  Kent looked at the fire and then looked at me. Looked at the fire and then looked at me. The heat pushed the two supporting sticks, and they swayed.

"Forget you sons of bitches," he said, and he sat down on a shovel as it was propped up against the wall. "I aint doin' it. I'm too pretty."

Kent was right. He was too damn pretty, and if I had looked like him, I would have bowed out too. But I never really had the looks. I mean, when I flip through photographs of myself from that time, I wished I knew how beautiful I was, but that's only because everything on me was fresh. When you are young, you don't have to be beautiful. You only have to be young, and that is enough, because you haven't yet earned your scars. Because I wasn't too pretty- and instead of looks I had courage- I didn't hesitate at all and went right on under that fire.

By the next round, the stick was eaten away and held on by a thin line of dark twig. Barbara went, and then Manny tried again, but he tripped backwards, so he was out too. It was down to me and Barbara. Nowadays confidence will make a modern girl go crazy when she sees it in someone else, but not then. We had enough enemies, and Barbara stood silently clapping for me, her perfectly full lips saying my name.

Even though the limbo stick was close to falling, I knew that I was going to do it anyway. I approached the flames, baptized in youth with that reckless feeling I had because I didn't have any responsibilities, like having two jobs and still being broke. Or having a teenaged daughter who is suicidal, and I don't know why. Because when I was 18 and, in that shed, my life was a ribbon of undriven highway in front of me.

But the stick came down on my bare knees, and my skin puckered and blistered instantly. Blinding, white-hot pain shot through my body. I jerked, and sparks bounced off my thighs and landed on the gasoline can, and everything slowed down again, and I watched the flame spreading like poured molasses down the sides of the can, and then Bang! I was suddenly plunged into a boiling, red soup.

The heat pressed in, relentless and probing. When I inhaled, I swallowed fire. But I found a small spot behind my ear, cool and clean. I dove into that safe space until it too dissolved in flame, and I rose up and up, and I looked down at my body that was me, and I saw the yellow fire's breath on my chin. The fire loved me. Consumed me. Reduced my pretty hair to ash.

And the shed was burning, burning to the ground with me inside it, and the skin on my neck peeled, pink and wet beneath black char. It was hard to be in the present moment when there was that much pain, and I looked to see if there was a future for me outside of this world of ash and flame, and immolating, I saw myself getting a degree, and my handsome husband and my beautiful daughters with their father's curly hair. I sat at our breakfast nook and stroked my Maine Coon cat.

The vision was ethereal. Too good to be true. And the steel drums played on as I squinted even farther into the future where the flames turned blue, and I gave my youngest daughter her very own box of matches.

They looked so pretty with their red tips and the glass powder shining on the side of the box like diamonds.

"Slow down," I told her as I showed her how to scratch the sulphur. "There is nowhere else to be. The world is one big limbo party on fire."

# 9

# THE RAPTURE OF ANNE MARIE ABBOT

Anne Marie Abbot sat in the parking lot, raking a golden crucifix back and forth along her necklace chain. It ripped beneath her fingers, sighing and vibrating like an opening zipper. She slid the cross partway into her mouth, and the cold metal shocked the tip of her tongue. She sucked the entire crucifix into her mouth, used the edge of her tongue to flip Jesus face down and explored his legs and arms and thorny crown as synthesized gospel music played on the radio.

Anne Marie tapped off the radio and exhaled. She pulled an oversized cardigan over her oversized blouse, hiding a tight body she thought was too prideful to admire. She walked, almost on tiptoe like a sneaky cartoon bandit, into the Baptist Rectory, down the front stairs, past the children's classrooms, following the smell of coffee and low murmurs until she reached the church parlor. Bile churned inside her stomach, and she suppressed a gag.

Anne Marie smoothed down the outdated layers of her frosted hair, cleared her throat quietly, and opened the door. Talk stopped, and five men, some in crumpled t-shirts and dirty jeans, some in nice trousers and buttoned up shirts, stopped stirring their coffees and looked up at her. A woman, the only woman there, smiled softly and patted the chair next to her.

Anne Marie slunk past the men and sat down.

"Hi, I'm Dottie, the woman said, extending her hand.

Her breasts jiggled warmly beneath her V-neck sweater.

Anne Marie wondered if Dottie was her real name.

"I'm Lora," Anne Marie said, using the name of a sorrowful woman in a romance novel she'd once read.

"Welcome," Dottie said, her hair bouncing above her still undulating breasts.

Uncomfortable, Anne Marie fiddled through her purse searching for a piece of gum. She pushed aside her checkbook and felt a little bit of shame that she had never caught on to fully using the debit card. Her fingernail jammed into the tip of an original black Chapstick without a lid, and she felt guilty that she was too thrifty to throw it out. She felt embarrassed by how her black shoes had a white scuff mark scraped along the side and that dark circles formed beneath her eyes because she hadn't been getting enough sleep.

Anne Marie felt ashamed of the way she put the crucifix in her mouth when she was nervous, and as a Protestant, ashamed of wearing a crucifix at all, and she kept Jesus faced down, his thorny-crowned forehead and stripped body nestled against her chest. She lowered her eyes to read scripture she'd written on an index card. "Cast all your anxieties on Him because He cares for you." Anne Marie felt ashamed again because though she was reading the word of God, nothing stirred in her heart.

Dottie caught her eye and smiled, wrinkles crinkling in the corners.

"Welcome to Kanawha County Chapter 3225 meeting of Sex Addicts Anonymous. My name is Dottie, and I'm a sex addict."

"Hello, Dottie," replied the men.

"Looks like we have a visitor," Dottie said, tilting her head towards Anne Marie. "Would you like to introduce yourself?"

Anne Marie dug her hands back in to her purse and rubbed the scripture card.

"Um."

She rubbed harder. No spirit reached her fingertips. The Holy Ghost did not appear. Anne Marie, without thinking, stuck the cross into her mouth. Metal struck her tongue. Anne Marie cupped her mouth so no one could see, and she pulled the suffering savior from between her teeth.

"My name is Anne Marie," she said.

She was not accustomed to lying.

"I mean, Lora."

"Shit," she said and tore a piece of the card.

She put her head in her hands. She was not accustomed to swearing.

Anne Marie, the pastor's wife, began to quietly cry.

"My name is Lora," she said. "I don't know who or what I am."

"Hello, Lora," they said.

She spent the rest of the meeting with her hands covering her face. Even after a man named Greg admitted picking up prostitutes. Even after Dottie said, with what appeared to be a hint of bragging, she'd slept with hundreds of men. Even after Maurice, the retired naval officer, hinted about touching young girls.

She listened to the cadence of their voices and analyzed the people by their sound. She was good at that. Knowing people. Finding out their sins. But she was also good at forgiving them too. Dottie wore her status as an addict with a bit of pride and spoke in strong, clipped phrases. Greg presented himself as plain and simple as his name. Maurice. What could she say about him? Something about him pricked her intuition. He was a wolf. A wolf lying in wait. He told his stories quietly, but with a mealy mouth. He never stopped moving his groin in slow circles or flicking the corner of his moustache with the tip of his white tongue. *Why was his tongue so white?* Anne Marie wondered. *A sign of infection?*

The meeting adjourned, and everyone got up from the table but Maurice, and Anne Marie could feel his stare. The hair on her forearms prickled to attention.

"Hey," he whispered and let his eyes fall to an envelope that he left on the table.

She knew he wanted her to pick it up, but she sat staring at it, afraid to touch it. He rose, and the front of his gray sweatpants brushed against the table, and she could see that he had half of an erection. He left with Greg, and soon the room emptied, except for Dottie who stayed behind to clean the coffee pot. She stacked the literature, placed it in a file cabinet, and locked it with a small key. Anne Marie stayed in her seat, eyeing the envelope.

Dottie put her hands on the back of Anne Marie's shoulders, and she felt the warmth of Dottie's comfort bleed through her thick clothing.

"You're going to be all right," she said.

Dottie's hands left her body, and with them went Dottie's warmth. Anne Marie shivered.

"I can't let you in here alone," Dottie said.

Anne Marie had been alone in a million churches a million times, had the key to her own church from which she could find innumerable ways to steal or vandalize, for the Lord had sought fit to bless her with a pastor for a husband.

A slice of light shined in from the hallway and illuminated the dusty floor. Bits of dirt, a chewed-on pencil, and a chunk of sugar donut made Anne Marie want to get out a mop and a broom. She eyed the envelope Maurice had left on the table. Something tingled in her navel. Checking to make sure Dottie wasn't watching, she snatched it up and tucked it into her purse.

She followed Dottie out, listening to their shoes squeak on the linoleum floor, listening to the junky rustle of the door opening, then slamming shut.

Once she was alone, Anne Marie tore a corner of the scripture card and put it in her mouth. She tasted cracker crumbs, bleeding ink, and the stale metal of old coins. The paper turned pasty in her mouth, but she chewed and swallowed the word of God.

She pulled out the envelope that Maurice had given her and opened the seal. It contained a flyer for a strip club called Genesis located on *412 Dogwood Street*. Anne Marie believed in prophecy, in numerology, and in signs and miracles. April 12th was Anne Marie's birthday, and Christ was said to be hung on slats made from the dogwood tree. She examined the photograph on the flyer, a woman with intense eyes looked right into Anne Marie's eyes.

☦

Anne Marie wiped down the kitchen counters. She sorted her husband's socks and scrubbed the inside of the toilet bowl with a long-handled brush. She caught a look at herself in the mirror. She wore her favorite outfit: a pink camisole top and faded blue jean shorts used inside and only for cleaning. The shorts sat low on the waist, and the camisole slid on her skin like silk. She'd never dare wear this in public, but Anne Marie suspected she had a sexy body. Her tight abs and petite form looked like the airbrushed magazine photos she'd seen on line at Kroger's. She wouldn't actually purchase magazines like these, but after checking left and right to see if anyone from church was nearby, she'd open Cosmo to see *10 Bedroom Secrets Revealed!* Glamour's, *Great Places to Have Public Sex!* And she'd compare herself to those gaunt women in golden eyeshades and think to herself, "I am more luxurious than that."

Her thighs were rich, and her bra was full, and because she was in between sizes, always spilling over a little. She hid all of this in modesty, and the only man to ever see her was The Pastor, but he kept the lights dim and his eyes closed.

Anne Marie removed her yellow gloves and washed the gritty latex off her fingers. She flicked at her breasts through the shelf bra, and her oversized nipples reached out for attention. She grabbed at them between her thumb and middle finger. Her eyes rolled back. Loneliness washed over her like water in a warm bath-- soothing and haunting at the same time.

She called her husband at work.

"Hello, Darling. I miss you," she said, her voice low and husky.

His ear didn't register that frequency. His nose couldn't smell sex. His mouth couldn't taste desire.

"I have a meeting this afternoon," he said. "Maybe I can get off early and we can go to the movies?"

He is a good and cheerful man, thought Anne Marie.

Anne Marie thought of the SAA meeting and how much worse the others had been. They were infinitely worse, criminally worse, and instead of exposure to these people fastening her shut and tamping her desire, something burst open in her as if the debauchery was infectious.

"Why don't you come home before your meeting and we can make love?"

Her heart pounded in her chest, and she held her breath.

"What?" The Pastor said. "That was rather forward, doncha' know? What's gotten into you?"

He chuckled nervously.

"I don't know," admitted Anne Marie.

She raised her camisole and looked at her naked breasts. Full and round, not a stretch mark in sight. She slid off her shorts.

She did not want to be doing this. She thought of the flyer for Genesis, and thinking of the dancers, she swayed her hips. She put her finger in her mouth and sucked like the woman on the flyer and was surprised at how it accented her cheekbones.

"Maybe on Friday," he said. "It's a finance meeting, so it's important."

Anne Marie climbed up on to the sink's long counter and reclined on to her left elbow. She especially did not want to be doing this.

"OK, maybe Friday," she said, reaching between her legs.

The Pastor talked about the men's Bible studies.

"I see," said Anne Marie.

The Pastor discussed the food pantry. Donations were down. How would they cover next Sunday's dinner?

"Mmmmm," said Anne Marie.

The Pastor brightened when he talked about the Cotillion, the rapture of the music, and his voice grew excited and quick.

"Yes, yes," said Anne Marie. "What else?"

The pastor's urgent breath pushed through the phone and took Anne Marie over the edge, and goose bumps traveled up and down her arms and legs. Her nipples hardened.

The pastor was laughing now, having told some funny story about Brother Tim that Anne Marie hadn't heard. Anne Marie laughed too, a languorous, honey of a laugh.

"That's nice," she said. She pulled on her shorts and shirt, smiling.

She caught hold of her reflection but didn't recognize her flush cheeks and parted mouth.

Anne Marie sighed and poured an equal amount of bleach and ammonia into the toilet bowl. She coughed as she submerged her touching hand, feeling the poison stinging a hangnail, burning her knuckles. Anne Marie counted backwards from 30. Then counted backwards again.

That night while washing dishes, her skin peeled off like wet paper.

☦

"My name is Maurice, and I'm a sex addict."

"Hello, Maurice."

"I've had a hard week," he said. "My wife's been out of town, and when she's gone it's harder for me to stay sober."

Sober, Anne Marie had gathered, was what they called resisting their unapproved sexual behavior. Anne Marie clutched at neckline of her blouse.

Maurice let out a sigh. She could smell the cigarettes on his breath.

"My baseline behaviors are masturbating, porn, and strip clubs."

At this he looked at Anne Marie and gave the slightest hint of a wink.

What had he been trying to do by giving her that flyer? Had he infiltrated the group with the express purpose of making everyone worse, like that slithering serpent enticing Eve to eat the apple?

The others nodded. The coffee maker sputtered. The heater kicked on.

"Porn's the hardest," Maurice said. "It's everywhere."

Anne Marie at 24 had never seen a full-on porno movie. In fact, the only pornography she'd seen was her grandfather's *Hustler* magazines she found beneath his bed. Anne Marie liked the dark, quiet, forbidden smell of her grandfather's bedroom. She liked the way the floor dipped in certain spots and how the linoleum's pattern had been worn off in front of his dresser. Bottles of cologne and aftershave lined up on his dresser like sentry. Old photographs of her grandmother were tucked into the frame of the mirror. Looking for solitude, Anne Marie crawled underneath the bed, arranging shoes in front of her body so she wouldn't be found. Her grandfather was a quiet man, and a bit aloof, but with warmth reserved only for her. He called her Lollipop. Because no other grandchild had a nickname, it felt right for her to be under his bed, among his hidden things.

The first pornographic image she saw was of a black haired, heavily eye-linered woman cupping her boobs, her tongue stretched out towards her own nipples. Anne Marie's heart jumped. Sweat filled her arm pits, and its acrid smell reached her nose. She flipped a page and saw delicately manicured nails holding open the folds of skin between her legs. Anne Marie's body chilled, filled with fear. She was afraid of getting caught looking, sure. But it was a deeper fear of… of what? She couldn't figure it out.

Perhaps it was terror over the power on those pages, the confident way the women looked right into the camera and could steal (she knew) any man away from her grandmother. Or maybe it was the vulnerability of private places made bare for men to look at and use. She was too young to understand, but a scared stitch surrounding sexuality began to knit within her.

Anne Marie left the meeting and made hot chocolate for The Pastor. She put two marshmallows in each mug, even though The Pastor never ate his. He always drank his hot chocolate quickly, and the two sugary pillows sat soggy and whole at the bottom of his empty mug, gone to waste.

"How was pottery class?" he asked.

"Fine," she said.

"What did you make tonight?"

"A vase," she said, but she could say whatever she wanted because she never brought anything home. The entire six weeks she'd been going to SAA, all her imaginary pottery was "in the kiln" and couldn't be accessed.

The Pastor slurped the last of his drink.

If he had any sin, thought Anne Marie, it was the sound his lips made as he motor-boated the side of every mug and every drinking glass.

"I'm going to preach about Tithing this Sunday. You think the congregation can handle a little more scripture this week?"

"Mmmm," Anne Marie said. "Sure."

The fluorescent light above the table flickered.

"I don't want to turn anyone off, especially a visitor, but the Bible needs to be preached."

"You're right," Anne Marie said.

"It's a fine balance," he said.

Anne Marie looked over at The Pastor. A bit of chocolate darkened the corners of his mouth.

She thought of crawling into his lap and licking his lips clean.

"I think I'll have Brother Tim preach soon. He's worked hard. He's earned it. And I think he's ready. If we can get the funds, I'd like to hire him full time."

Anne Marie handed The Pastor a paper napkin. He wiped his lips without tidying the corners. *But still, he's a good man*, thought Anne Marie. He wasn't a pulpit hoarder, or easily weakened by jealousy or fear. He was giving the dynamic young intern, Brother Tim, a chance at the spotlight.

*And he probably hopes he'll do well,* Anne Marie thought. That's how good of a man The Pastor is.

Anne Marie pushed her marshmallow to the bottom of the mug with a spoon and held it there. She thought of her grandfather drowning kittens in the above ground swimming pool, how he'd held them down in a sack and how she had watched from behind the bushes without doing anything at all to help them. Her grandfather, how she idolized him and feared him both.

She thought about those magazines under his bed. How his tidy grandmother must have known, must have accepted them, and what did that mean?

"I'm going to send some emails," Anne Marie said, excusing herself.

"Alrighty, then," The Pastor said, and kissed his wife on the cheek.

He reached over and stroked her hair. Gave her another kiss on the cheek. He programmed the coffee pot for the morning and put in a fresh filter and six heaping spoonfuls of Organic, Fair-Trade grounds. The Pastor was a kind man and thought globally. He used filtered water to fill the basket and set out Anne Marie's favorite mug. He arranged a clean spoon and the sugar bowl beside it, all the while humming a tender song Anne Marie recognized as "The Old Rugged Cross." She slid her crucifix into her mouth and waited for The Pastor to head to bed.

Anne Marie sent a few emails. Anne Marie searched for craft projects. Anne Marie tiptoed down the hall and listened outside of the bedroom door to The Pastor's warm snore. She crept back to the computer and typed one word into the search engine: sex.

A message popped on screen:

YOUR CURRENT SAFESEARCH SETTING FILTERS OUT RESULTS THAT MIGHT

RETURN ADULT CONTENT. TO VIEW THOSE RESULTS AS WELL, CHANGE YOUR SAFESEARCH SETTING

She turned off the SafeSearch and typed the word again. Magazine articles about health benefits of sex, definitions of intercourse, and other educational content popped up. Anne Marie looked at her blinking curser. She cracked her knuckles then typed in: Pornography.

PORNOGRAPHY: WIKIPEDIA

FREE PORN VIDEOS.

SEX MOVIES

PORNOGRAPHY AND WOMEN.

She wasn't titillated by women, so it wasn't like cheating, was it? This was research. This was education. Her search resulted in GIFS of women in bikinis stretched out on cars, overhead shots of blondes and brunettes and red heads looking up at cameras.

Anne Marie's looked over her shoulder and listened for The Pastor. Her palms grew clammy. She clicked on the first link. It took her to a flawless brunette with sun tanned thighs wearing too small of a bra crawling on her hands and knees towards the camera. Anne Marie felt sort of sad and a little sick in her body. She did not want to view her fellow women in this way. So Anne Marie googled Pornography Men.

VIDEOS FOR MEN: SEXY WOMEN SHOWER FOR YOU

HOT GAY MEN IN SPEEDOS

Anne Marie boiled inside. Where were HOT MEN SHOWER FOR YOU? Anne Marie checked to make sure she knew how to clear her search history. She typed in Bananas. Clicked on the first link. Then cleared her history.

Anne Marie clicked. And clicked. And clicked again. She learned the words that brought up the images that interested her and typed words that she'd never said out loud. Words like: Pussy. Cock. Tits. She felt weary, disturbed, tired. Titillated. Excited. Energized. In her searching, she learned a new language. Foot job. Squirter. MILF. Tadgers. She learned what words were coded for gay porn. In general, it was the word "boys." Legal boys. Pretty boys. Boys on leash. She learned how to avoid S & M. Don't click anything related to leather or gag ball or plug.

At 3 AM Anne Marie put the crucifix in her mouth, reached beneath her robe and tapped between her legs. Before coming, she cleared her internet history. She went to church the next morning feeling raked over and tired. She prayed that God would save her. She took off her cross because she felt unworthy to wear it. She felt guilty for taking it off, so she put it back on again. It was Sunday, and giving sermons always boosted his libido, so The Pastor wanted to make love that night. Anne Marie put him off and stayed up late clicking, tapping, and clearing.

Monday she went to SAA.

Tuesday she cut out a felt manger scene for Sunday school.

Wednesday, Anne Marie had an idea. An epiphany, really. She thought to type in "Porn for Women."

The computer screen glowed.

COUPLES EROTICA, NEW STORIES AND PICS POSTED DAILY

ARE YOU GETTING ENOUGH TONGUE? SANDY IS. CLICK FOR CUNNILINGUS

FORGET HAIRY AND FAT PORN STARS, SQUEEKY CLEAN PAUL SOAPS UP

FIELD GUIDE MEN RECLINE IN NATURE, HOT GUYS WITH NICE EYES.

Then,

HANDSOME HUSBANDS.

Her pupils dilated. She clicked the link. There she saw men in khakis and button-down shirts, opened all the way down showing trails of hair that lead the eye. The men held roses. Puppies. Glasses of champagne. Anne Marie sucked in a breath of air.

On Sunday, she was scheduled for sacred dance for the 10 AM and 11:30 worship service. Anne Marie pulled up her white tights, beginning with the dainty point of her toe then stretching up past her toned calves and delicate knees. She paused and turned her leg to the right and the left, admiring the curves and lines. She moved her hand across the sheer nylon and gave a tug. It felt good in the body to touch and stretch the fabric over her dancer's legs. She was mindful and attentive. Christian contemplation in its purest form, and since she'd quit praying, she missed the practice of finding God in the mundane.

When she leaned forward to put on her leotard, the crucifix pulled on its chain and tapped against her nose. "No sucking on crucifix" had become a base-line behavior, and Anne Marie did not take the bait. She put a loose shirt over her leotard and tights and walked to stage left, waiting her turn to worship. The lights dimmed and the music rose. Anne Marie spun on to the stage, her arms lifted in the air in praise. She pulled upward on to her toes and stretched her long body toward God.

In dance, Anne Marie realized she ached for Him, longed for Him. Her body wanted Him, and she felt an energy drain from her navel down to her pubic bone. Anne Marie, now on her knees, arched her back and circled both her arms to the left, then back around her body. Her rib and pelvis bones poked through her leotard until her graceful arms had come back around the other side of her body. Anne Marie recognized her lust and that her God was the object, and shame slammed down hard upon her. She leaned even further onto her knees until the bones ground against the hard stage floor. She felt an urge, no a need, to wipe her hair along the floor, and she did. But this was not enough, and a small quickening rose in her abdomen, as painful as a tickle that she knew would not go away until she had done what was put into her mind to do. As the last note of the song faded, she hid her face in the crook of her elbow. When she was sure she could not be seen, she splayed her tongue flat and dragged it across the floor. When she closed her mouth, she could feel small grains of dirt and a thin line of hair, which she did not allow herself to remove. Anne Marie could feel her breath bouncing back to her from the floor, could hear the pounding of her heart. Smell the waxy scent of liturgical candles. The congregation sat mute and still in the pews, for this was a new song they had never sung.

She searched the front row for The Pastor in his usual spot and found him clutching his Bible, mouth agape.

Finally, Brother Tim cleared his throat. "Amen," he said and clapped. Given permission to respond, the congregation joined in. On and on the applause echoed off the stained glass. The people stood on their feet. Some jumped with the Holy Ghost fire. The collection plate was passed, and quickly filled, the dollar bills piled to overflowing.

Anne Marie looked out into the congregation and saw Brother Tim wiping his eyes. She saw The Pastor look at her with a queer smile. Anne Marie ran offstage in the opposite direction from The Pastor and locked herself in the women's bathroom. She did not dress in a long skirt and a long sweater and sit in the front pew to watch The Pastor preach like she usually did. Instead, she gathered her clothes in her arms and ran directly to the car. She pulled out her notebook and under "base line behaviors to avoid," she wrote the words: "Sacred dance."

☦

"My name is Dottie and I'm a sex addict."

"Hello Dottie."

"My baseline behaviors are no texting or emailing with men, no calling men on the phone when it's not business, no porn."

"Oh, and no masturbation," Dottie added with a chuckle.

Anne Marie learned that to the addict, masturbation engaged the disturbed fantasy life and was like a gateway drug that could lead to all sorts of other behaviors. Anne Marie understood the slippery slope of sin, and she was terrified to think how she'd started SAA because of how much she wanted sex and how little The Pastor required it, and she didn't know what to do with this gap. And now in mere weeks she'd moved on to porn and masturbation. She was not like Jesus. She could not be with the tax collectors and prostitutes and maintain her purity. Yet she felt that she needed the help more than ever and couldn't afford to quit the group.

"Tried to sneak that one by?" Maurice asked, grinning.

"Of course," said Dottie.

Anne Marie looked around at the laughing faces. Dottie's jaw wobbled, and Maurice's forehead rippled with wrinkles. Anne Marie would laugh too, if nothing else but to not stand out, but the thought of confessing her sins made her throat squeezed tight as if someone had his knee on her neck. She couldn't get enough air, so she pulled at the neck of her blouse. The smell of cheap coffee made her stomach sour. Anne Marie brought her crucifix to the tip of her nose and let it fall back down to her cardigan. She slid the crucifix onto her tongue and felt Jesus' knees poke at the roof of her mouth. She worried that even if she didn't tell anyone her dark deeds, they could be seen and sensed on her fingers. Her face grew red and hot and blots of black obstructed her vision until she completely blacked out.

When she came to, she was on the floor of church, Dottie, Greg, and Maurice looking down at her. She could not help but think, "This is what it looks like to be underneath them during sex," and she felt as if just by thinking the thought or even being here, she was sinning. She tried to sit up.

"Lie still," Dottie said. "We called an ambulance."

"No," Anne Marie said. She wouldn't be caught dead at an SAA meeting, and she willed herself to her feet and made it out to the car before the ambulance arrived. But on the boulevard where she should have turned left, Anne Marie kept on driving. She headed for Genesis. It was calling to her, tugging at her breastbone. She would casually drive by, have a look at the kind of people who went inside. Face this fear head on so that it would quit suffocating her, quit shaming her, quit making a fool of her.

Across the street at the gas station, she filled up, even though her tank was nearly full, and then parked her car next to the air pump on the side of the station. She left the engine running so that she could hear gospel radio. There were no windows to the club, only a solid metal door, and aside from the neon sign flashing Genesis! Genesis! Genesis! gave no hint as to the life behind it. The door opened and a regular looking man in khakis and a button-down polo exited. Anne Marie watched men walk in, fixing their hair with fingers as makeshift combs. Men in suits. Men in jeans and ball caps.

Only the few men with beards looked like perverts up to no good. Facial hair always looked pervy to Anne Marie. Even on portraits of Jesus. Made them look like they had something to hide around the mouth. Otherwise, these men looked like brothers and uncles, the butcher at Kroger's, and maybe if she squinted, Brother Tim.

A Jeep careened into the parking lot, made a jerky turn past the parking spots out front, and came to an abrupt stop at the side of the building. A woman got out of the car wearing jeans, a thick sweater, and oversized hoop earrings. She slung a duffel bag over her shoulder, tossed in her keys, and swung open a side door. Thumping music pulsed from inside, and though Anne Marie craned her neck to peek inside, she could see nothing but painted grey cinder block. Anne Marie slumped back into her seat. She drummed her hands on the steering wheel. She opened her Bible, then closed it. What was the point of her being here? She knew that it would be revealed to her if she just opened her heart to knowing.

Anne Marie considered her own dancing and felt an instant prick of shame about her last performance. She missed the body movement, missed the feel of the costume fabric on her skin, and something within her stirred, and with great care, she retrieved her costume from the truck and slid the leotard and tights onto her body. She covered up with a long cardigan and crossed the street to the strip club parking lot and cut the engine.

The side door opened again, and music thumped through the open crack. Two women leaned against the wall, lit a cigarette, and shared it between them. Anne Marie watched as the red tip of the cigarette glowed bright, then faded, with each puff. Anne Marie used to smoke. Before she met The Pastor. Before she met Jesus. The addiction called to her in that moment. She wanted a drag, a hit, a long slow inhale of smoke that she could feel in her lungs and in her throat.

Anne Marie sucked in a breath and pulled hard on the car's silver handle, swung open the car door and walked over to the two women. One of them yawned and showed a silver filling.

"Can I bum a smoke?" Anne Marie asked.

The woman looked her up and down. Anne Marie held out her hand.

"Who are you?" she said but began to rummage around in her purse.

She found the pack and held out a cigarette. Anne Marie smelled her perfume, surprisingly clean and breezy like the dancer's young skin. Anne Marie took the cigarette and held it in her hands.

"Got a light?"

"Christ," the woman said. "Want me to smoke it for you too?"

"I've got it covered," Anne Marie said and leaned in.

Anne Marie sucked in the smoke. It was as she remembered. Hot and rough on the throat followed by the instant head rush of nicotine. She swayed a little to the left.

"So who are you?" the woman asked again.

Anne Marie picked a piece of tobacco off her tongue.

"Trinity," she said, buzzed on nicotine. "I'm the new dancer."

Anne Marie wanted to take it back, run to her car and call The Pastor, but she surprised herself by making a perfect smoke ring O.

"Yeah, well," the woman said. "There's always a new dancer."

"I'm Gemma and that's Rachael."

Rachel yawned again and flicked the butt of her cigarette against the wall. It bounced, creating a festive spray of red ash. She opened the door, and Gemma walked through. She paused in the doorway and said over her shoulder to Anne Marie, "You coming or not?"

Anne Marie nodded, took a final drag off her cigarette and flicked it between her middle finger and thumb and watched as the butt bounced twice, spraying orange flakes of flame on the concrete. Once inside, they passed the grey cinder blocks and followed the corridor to the end where a large dressing room had only a half-closed curtain for a door.

"You talk to Ray yet?" Rachel asked.

Anne Marie nodded.

"I gotta tell you," Rachael said, "The leotard is retro and cool right now, but the tights have got to go."

She dug through a dresser drawer and produced a pair of sheer white thigh highs she tossed in Anne Marie's direction.

"Here. Wear these."

Anne Marie grabbed them but hesitated on changing until Gemma pulled off her coat to reveal bare breasts with rhinestones glued on to the nipples in a spiral pattern. She stepped out of her pants, and her panties were fringed with crystals so that when she walked, she tinkled like a chandelier being dusted.

Rachel threaded her legs through a fantasy suit made entirely of thin, metal straps. Her bra was a steel concoction that shot propane out of each hammered nipple that she lit off stage so that she could enter in style, tits ablazin'.

Anne Marie peeled off her leotard and tights in one quick pull, but slid back into the leotard slowly. The fabric band tugged between her legs without the benefit of tights to soften the touch. She stretched thigh highs over her legs and began searching for a pair of heels.

"We gotta go," Rachel said. "Ray's down the hall." And the two of disappeared out onto the main floor.

The room was crammed full of props and creams and wigs and gadgets and boas. A film of dusty face powder settled on the vanity, and the surfaces were cluttered with musk- scented lotions, errant hair clips, and eyeshadow palates. A bra made of candy hung from the arm of a chair. She found a small, filmy, white skirt slung over the arm of a chair and stepped into it.

She leaned over the counter and slid purple eyeshade across her lids, rubbed small circles of blush along the apples of her cheeks. She rummaged through a jewelry box on the counter, vaguely aware of diseases like hepatitis and gonorrhea but shrugged and glued on a pair of false eyelashes. She dug through nipple clamps and belly button rings and clip on earrings that dangled like silver waterfalls.

Anne Marie felt fear. But this was altogether a different kind of thing than she'd experienced looking at porn at home, or what she felt as a little girl under her grandfather's bed. Then it had been a fear of things outside of her control. How women acted. How men behaved. What beautiful women looked like and how she compared. But now, Anne Marie's heart began to quake over her own behavior.

How had she gotten here? And why didn't she just leave?

A white, feathered mask was tucked into the corner of a wall sized mirror. Anne Marie picked it up and stroked it before fitting it over her face. She took a long look at herself in the full-length mirror. She turned and glanced over her shoulder at the back of her thighs. Trinity was flawless.

Emboldened by her mask, she walked down the hallway towards the music until the hallway split off. On the left, was a private room with a small stage made of painted plywood, and to the right a set of stairs led up to the main room, sectioned off only by a black curtain. Anne Marie ascended the stairs, feeling how tightly her calf muscles moved in high heeled shoes. She paused at the peak and opened a small bit of the curtain. Chairs with cushions covered in black vinyl lined up before the main stage. Thumping bass blasted from speakers mounted on the walls. A tiny girl, about five foot one, was dusting and buffing table surfaces with her feathered panties, shimmying a few feet at a time as she worked.

Rachael was on stage, her nipples recently extinguished. Men tucked dollar bills into her costume. Assorted men surrounded the stage and populated the small, circular tables around the room as Rachael slipped out of her metal bra.

It surprised Anne Marie that some of the men in the back played cards and hardly looked at the women at all. It disturbed her even more to find women patrons, accompanying their boyfriends or friends for a night out. Hired women pranced among the tables, bending their elbows on to the sticky surfaces, raising their heels as they giggled. She watched Rachael lead one man by the hand in to another room. Maurice had taught her what this meant at the Pink Pony, and Anne Marie followed to watch.

As she walked, men called out to her.

"What's your name, Baby?"

"Come sit over here."

Walking downtown, this behavior would have frightened her, made her uncomfortable. In this context, she felt a surge of power, and with her back erect, she ignored him.

The "Private dance" room held one, long, sectional couch, and more than one man and dancer pair were in there, men sitting on their hands while girls moved slowly around them, their joints and cheap high heeled shoes popping at the pressure points. Air in the small room didn't circulate, and it smelled of beer and sweat and perfume. Rachel pointed to a seat at the end of the couch, and the man sat down. She ran her hands up and down her body, hooked her thumbs into the strings of her panties. She turned and looked at the man over her left shoulder. Rachael lifted her head at the man, opened her mouth and then bit her lip. She gave him a hungry smile that looked like she wanted to eat him. She noticed Anne Marie watching and called to her with a seductive finger. Anne Marie shook her head, but Rachael pranced over to her and laced both of her hands through Anne Marie's fingers and pulled her, wiggling and slithering, over to the man.

"Her dance is $20," Rachael said. "And you can tip, can't you?"

"Well!" the man said, smiling. He leaned in, and in doing so, his face came into a strip of light, and Anne Marie recognized the man as Brother Tim.

Anne Marie froze, her face turning hot and flushed.

But her face was hidden behind the mask, and Brother Tim made no signs of recognizing her. Anne Marie began to dance, swaying her body timidly. She watched Brother Tim's face, noticed how eagerly he leaned in, and how at home he appeared. He was utterly without shame, the same shame that had been pressing in on Anne Marie for weeks. For years, even.

Rachael let go of Anne Marie's hands, put her hands around Brother Tim's neck, leaned over him, and said into his ear, "Keep your hands to yourself and sit back, relax, and enjoy." She looked at Anne Marie and nodded.

Rachael turned around, bent her knees and popped her ass into the air and jiggled it in Tim's face.

"Mmmmm," he said.

"Do you like that?" Rachael cooed.

"Oh yeah," he said.

"How about this?" Rachael asked and began running her fingers down Anne Marie's body.

"I like," he said.

The sentence fragment bothered Anne Marie. It was a sneaky intruder that spread and stained her insides. She felt sick and disgusted with herself. She felt disgusted with Tim, she had stripped him of his Christian title now, watching her with his small eyes. Anne Marie went, as she did in times of great stress and struggle, to God.

In her heart she began to pray and praise, and Anne Marie began to move her body in generous, swirling circles.

Anne Marie felt a tremor in her body, and she recognized this as the Holy Spirit within her. She raised her arms in supplication, fell on her knees in repentance. She prayed with her body and felt the Divine in the quickening of her heart, in the way her skirt swayed on her hips.

She prayed for Tim with the laying on of hands. She interceded for him in tongues. Still on the floor, she crawled over to him and prayed over his feet and his shins and his knees. She blessed his thighs with her palms, warmed his abdomen with her worship. Tim put his hands in her hair, and she let him. She rolled her head back in passion and Anne Marie lost herself in this holy threesome: God, herself, and Tim.

"Take off your mask," Tim whispered into her ear, and the desperation in his voice made everything else fade away. Tim, so good with the youth group. Tim, so quick with a joke. Tim, with his hardened biceps and thin waist.

"Please?" he asked.

Anne Marie took off her mask and handed it to him. She saw recognition in his eyes, and she poured blessing upon the crown of his head, touching his face and cheeks with her palm. He let out a moan, a long sighing gasp.

Anne Marie, startled, opened her eyes and saw him cupping his crotch with his hands, a small dark spot beginning to bleed into the fabric of his khaki pants. Tim covered himself with his jacket. He wrenched a wallet from his pocket and pulled out all of the bills that he had, holding the fistful of dollars out to her. He looked like a frightened boy making his first purchase by himself. An ice cream cone, maybe. A matchbox car.

They blinked at one another, Tim and his wet khakis. Anne Marie and her bare thighs.

The money shook in his trembling hands, and the bills looked familiar to her, like the wads of cash piled up in the collection plate. Anne Marie grabbed the bills, and they felt hot to the touch, as if warmed by his lust. She swiveled on her heels towards the dressing room, her feet quickening until she hit full run. Tim did not call after her.

Anne Marie kept running, but she tripped on some taped down wire and split her lip on the edge of a table.

Rachel helped her up, and they walked back into the dressing room.

"Someone you know, huh?" she said. "It's bound to happen, and it can be a real kick in the crotch."

Rachel dabbed at Anne Marie's lip with a tissue.

"Wait 'till it's one of your friend's dads."

Rachel laughed. "Why don't you hang out here for a few, and I'll let you know when he's gone, and you can come back out."

Anne Marie's cell phone rang from somewhere in the dressing room. It was The Pastor's ring tone, a synthesized gospel classic. She held the phone in her hand for a moment, smeared a wide smile on her face before pressing the green icon.

"Hello, Honey," she said into the phone. "I'm going to be a little late. I have to wait for the mug to dry before I put on a second layer of glaze."

☦

When she arrived home that night, Anne Marie saw Tim's car in the driveway. Had he come to confess? Or to play righteous pastor and say that he had seen her car in a strip club parking lot and saved her from iniquity? Her hands shook as she slid her key into the front door, but it was already unlocked. Tim and The Pastor were sitting on the couch, the smell of fresh coffee and Danish sweetened the air. Anne Marie's stomach knotted.

"There she is," The Pastor said, and Anne Marie swallowed hard.

"I'm sorry," she said.

"Oh, it's no interruption. We're just going over financials," The Pastor said. "Trying to figure out how to hire this one full time," he said, thrusting a thumb in Tim's direction.

Tim did not look up.

Anne Marie smiled but pretended to fiddle with something in her purse.

"Wouldn't that be nice?" she said, and she saw Tim's body relax.

Anne Marie locked the bathroom door, undressed, and retrieved the ammonia from beneath the cabinet. She stepped into the shower, carrying the bundle of Tim's bills with her. She washed each piece of money with lye soap, pressing the clean ones and fives and tens and twenties on the clear, sliding door in tidy rows. Each dollar represented a prayer she had offered, an act of worship each, and the stall was covered top to bottom with her gifts.

Not all offerings come to Christ on a plate.

# 10

# ORANGE SEXY ORANGE

There is an orange in my hand. I feel its dimples and its wet skin and when I press my nail into the flesh, the tangy energy inside is released. It's clean and antiseptic and I carry something citrus in my left hand every day. Could be lemon, too. Could be lime, too. Today it is an orange. There is a pack on my back, slung over my left shoulder. It brushes along my torso and when I walk it bumps against my rib and pinkens my skin. In the bag I've got a computer, black wire, some lipstick sexy and a comb. A banana muffin wrapped in a napkin disintegrates with every step I take because the wire sexy and the lipstick rub against it. Reduce it to crumbles.

There is a mole on my cheek below my left eye. When I was ten, my mother darkened it with an eyebrow pencil. Sexy she'd say. Wear these shoes she'd say. They show off your shapely foot. Add lipstick and a gloss.

Almost home and it's no accident the neighbor's hose comes alive jerking and spitting like a cobra at my ankles. Bill grins and continues to turn the screw and the pressure builds and rises and not being one to run away sexy I step on the rubber with my heeled shoes but the brass end bites my leg. Water turns my blouse see-through. Drenches my hair. He looks at me. I look at him. Drip drip drop the hose. Purple, black, blood bruise filling sexy like a kiss, sexy like a bite. Soaking wet curl points to my mouth. Good day I say to the neighbor leave him wanting more. Know sexy he's watching me walk away. Glad I'm wearing these shoes, squeezing this fruit. Look over my shoulder. Drip. Squeeze.

Locked the screen door behind me. Locked the storm door behind me. Roll the orange in my palms. The doorbell rings.  Tug fruit out of snug skin. The doorbell rings. Pull apart the flesh in 12 tidy sections. A knock on the door. Stroke my tender rib and eye the juicy parcels on the counter lined up and waiting. Cut open a can of asparagus with strong sexy pumps of the wrist pumps of the wrist pumps of the wrist and pounding on the door nibble sexy the pointed tips of twenty-four thin, limp asparaphallis sexy.

Hello the neighbor says waving through the window watching me eat. Black wire coils within. There are lemons in my hand. They're clean and antiseptic and my bag rubs up against my rib. I watch through the glass. Roll lime through my palm. He stops knocking and watches me eat. His hand frozen at a fist on my window. He's still and this is what I've been sexy holding out for.

I open the door. My clothes are wet. My eyes are brown. Juice from the orange drips sexy on my chin. His hair is red and curly. Red brow, red beard, a forest of red chest hairs. I point to the couch and in comes Bill like a red flame, a ball of fire with that red hair. A pomegranate. An apple.

He ignores the couch. Comes at me gape mouthed like a fish. Like a pickerel, big wide smile. I return his kiss sexy smiling like guppy, lick like lizard, tongue like fire.

You taste like orange, he says. Clean, he says. Bill tastes like mildew. Algae and watery grave.  Let's get you out of these wet clothes, he says. Cut right to the chase, I say. He smiles and I see a glint of silvery hook in his cheek. You're a stunning girl, Bill says. I'm a woman, I say and unfasten the button of his jeans with my teeth. You sure are, he says.

White cotton panties caught at my ankles, white cotton bra with a little red cherry at the clasp. His fingers fumble and give up. He scoops me out of the cups and rests them on top of the underwire. He comes. I choke. I walk to the counter, stuff orange peel between my teeth and gums. Look to Bill and reveal a wide, orange smile. You know the kind. Bill laughs and jingles his belt buckle closed.  Hook is out of his mouth and snagged on my own lip. Bound in my mother's corset of orange sexy orange.

# 11

# ZEROS AND ONES AT THE FUNK YOU FESTIVAL

It's just after noon, and the first act of the *Funk You Festival* takes the stage. It's a white guy from rural Appalachia performing rap to a home crowd. The songs are about buttery biscuits and listening to metal music in a van while getting stoned. Write what you know. I got in for free with my boyfriend because even though he's getting too old for it, he's carrying equipment, plugging in cords and taping down wires. In between, he's vaping with the bands and getting them American lagers and pre-made sandwiches from the VIP area.

Every now and then he smuggles me a draft in a red solo cup.

There's not much of a crowd yet. More will come as the sun starts to fade. For now, it's as though the rapper is doing a sound check. He keeps forgetting the words. Says he's trying to keep it clean for the kids. But when he spits, it sounds smooth. He enunciates, and I hear every word. I recognize the places around town he mentions, the levee where I smoked my first cigarette, the holler down Spring Road where my best friend lived and I learned how to curl my hair. The memories soothe me, help me to relax, but my boyfriend comes back with a free bag of chips and asks me why I look so sad. Before I can reassure him that I'm fine, he plants me with a quick kiss and darts back into the VIP area.

I notice a boy, maybe 6 or 7, lining Transformer toys in a perfectly straight line along the amphitheater step. Primary colors in soldier formation. He wears a black Batman shirt, black shorts, trendy skater shoes. Has one of those haircuts like you'd see in the 40's with long, sleek bangs that hang over one eye, shaved at the neck. Cute kid. Adorable, even. I'd engage with him, but I'm so tired.

I've had two weeks of 12-hour shifts, and I just want to rest my body, turn off my brain, forget all of the runny eggs and ketchup bottles I delivered to hundreds of tables, all while fending off the leering manager who thinks that I find his groping hands flattering. I have another shift tomorrow, but today is mine, and I'm working to consciously relax my shoulders, to breathe through my diaphragm, and let it all go.

The boy in the Batman shirt is running in front of the stage, showing off. He's kind of kick-boxing, kind of dancing. He's looking at me as he runs. Like everyone else, he wants to extract what I have to give. He wants my attention. I exhale long and slow, try to remember what that free internet Masterclass told me about overextending myself. But it's no use.

I glance behind me at the boy's parents. Just being here with their kid makes them liberal. Woke. They are sitting in their folding chairs, a cooler beside them. Blanket bunched at their feet. Dad is wearing last year's *Funk You Festival* t-shirt. He has long, curly black hair, starting to gray, pulled back beneath a thick headband, hiding a receding hairline, I think. He's wearing circular sunglasses and the same skater shoes as his son. Looks cool as hell. The mom's sundress rides high, far above her knees. It's held up with skinny straps, the kind you could imagine disintegrating like spider webs, the kind that doesn't allow you to wear a bra underneath. The crowd is so sparse she has plenty of room, and she stretches her long body, arms waving above her head, making her sundress even shorter, and it doesn't seem to matter to her whether anyone is looking or not. She's moving sensually to music about biscuits while I'm thinking, *I could make love to a properly made biscuit, too.* Flaky layers. Home-made apple butter, slathered thick. Dripping down the sides.

The boy is in front of me, still reaching out for my attention. A headache is starting to form behind my right eye, but I'm not the kind to withhold, and it doesn't cost me a dime. I look at the boy, and I smile. His face lights up, and he adds gun shooting gestures and a few "Pow Pow's" to his dance-walk.

The next band takes the stage. These four guys look like they could have been my friends in college. They're wearing khaki pants and t-shirts with dead musicians on them. David Bowie. Tom Petty. Prince. This band's been around a while, and their playing is tight. The act that follows is also all men, except this time there are six instead of four.

There's a horn player, and he's my favorite part so far. I get to feeling like I could straddle the notes and ride them like a rocket, scream right out into space where I could trace the horns of Taurus, graze the bow of Orion, lie down and sleep in the cold blue light of the stars. A strange sensation begins to form in my body, a sort of vertigo, a dropping into myself, and I close my eyes, feeling the music vibrate my bones. I don't recognize the feeling as "rest" until the very moment it is interrupted by a tapping on my shoulder.

My eye lids feel heavy, so heavy, but I open them, and it's the little boy standing in front of me. Up close I can see that he's wearing hair gel and his eyelashes are thick and fringed. There is a reason people call some boys "Little Men." He is half boy and half little man, dressed like his father — so hip, so cool — but there's the Batman logo and the toys his mom packed in a bag sewn from an old pair of jeans.

Other than the famous book title, no one ever calls little girls "Little Women," though the acts men do in private do so wordlessly. The scars follow us to adulthood, where we are then called "Girls," and we lug the weight of our wounds into biscuit stores and music festivals and every single relationship we enter thereafter.

The boy is standing so close to me that I can smell his breath, milky and sweet.

"Hi," I say, and he runs back to his father who is rummaging around in his cooler.

The amphitheater is starting to fill. The boy's mother had to move in front of the stage to have room for her hula hoop, and the father is holding a fresh craft beer and starting to wobble. I take another nibble from a gummy my boyfriend brought, but I can't feel it. It's like the high is jammed somewhere in my cerebellum, just out of reach.

The boy is moving back and forth in front of me like a shark in a small tank, and when he gets to the invisible end, he doubles back the other way. Back and forth he swims, all the while, kicking and punching at the air. It's like he's screaming, "Look at me, Look at me."

I look at him. I look at him.

I am watching the band, and I am watching the boy. The boy stops running and begins to walk, strutting now as he passes. He's a few feet away when he looks over his shoulder and directly into my eyes. He pauses.

He has great posture, shoulders back, looks like a frat boy with that haircut, with his lips turned up in a cunning smile. He's a pro. So suave, so debonair.

Slowly, deliberately, while his right eye remains perfectly open, his left eye shuts.

A wink.

I see the future man in the childhood body, and I am startled. Uneasy.

"Oh," I say, but no one is there to listen.

An uncomfortable heat floods my face. I look to see if his father is watching, but he is swaying to the music, eyes closed. I search for his mother, and she is still dancing. Alone. Happy. Content. The boy hits the invisible edge of his tank and circles back. I look at the ground until he passes and then move to the opposite side of the amphitheater. He is a boy. I guess around six or seven years old. He has the power to awaken fear in me.

The next band is another bunch of guys, but they let a woman sing back up. It's been all men on the docket all day. It's all men throughout the evening. I wonder if anyone catches this or if I'm the only one. I'm half incredulous and half relieved. My boyfriend likes the lady singers, and while he's a good man, I can quickly get to obsessing when I think about them meeting backstage- his lips wrapping around the tip of the same joint a sexy singer wet with her pouty mouth. I imagine it like some sort of kiss they'd shared behind the stage. Behind my back.

He doesn't do much ogling, but after he's had a few drinks, he can get to staring, and I get to feeling fat and unattractive, and I start to feel shame for thoughts of making love to a biscuit.

My headache has spread, and I press my temples to ease the pain. I can hear my pulse in my ears, and I think I may be falling asleep in little 5 second bursts. I want to go home, lie down in my bed with a damp rag on my forehead, but there's the headlining act, and then my boyfriend has to strike the stage, and I get to help by carrying festival detritus like cords and masking tape and unsold t-shirts to the performers' vans. A muscle in my right shoulder spasms at the thought of carrying one more goddamn thing ever, ever again.

The headliner is on stage now, and with every song, he takes off more and more clothing. He has the torso of a middle-aged man. Small, pasty breasts. Swelling stomach. Sporadic tufts of hair sprouting here and there. The crowd is going wild. Women are crushing the stage to get closer to him. Closer to all that swagger. All that confidence. I admit, I'm drawn in too. The mother is holding the boy as she sways to the music, her pheromones oozing out into the night sky, drifting their way towards the performer's nose. An invisible beacon draws his eyes to her moving body, and there is a look on his face, one the boy does not yet understand, but the mother knows, and she nods, a tiny, imperceptible movement that the boy feels in his chest.

The men are nodding to the thump of the bass, unthreatened. He looks like them. Maybe worse than they do. They can see themselves on stage in his place, a crowd of women at their feet.

Now is the big finale. All that remains of the performer's clothing are his breakaway pants, and with a single tug, they are off. He is wearing a cowbell codpiece. As he thrusts his hips, we hear the tinny echo of percussion. They moan along, yeah, yeah, oooh, yeah.

It's all so binary, the parts that men are taught to play, the parts that women play too. But the lines are starting to blur, and he is fucking all of the men now too as they line up at his feet, cheering and giving their consent.

The performer is prowling the stage, back and forth, like a lion in a cage. Like a shark in a tank. Back and forth he goes. When he gets to the invisible end, he doubles back the other way. Two girls in bikinis, hair teased high, flank the stage. This brings the female performer count of the entire festival to three. They're each straddling a confetti cannon, and at the final note, the festival comes to an orgasmic end. Rainbow colored flecks of tissue paper burst into the air and suspend there for a moment or two while the crowd cheers. The confetti floats down and begins to stick on the crowd's sweaty and naked skin. One pink triangle alights at the corner of a woman's lip-glossed mouth, and I can't take my eyes off of her until she removes it with one long, sexy, stroke of her middle finger.

When the fun dies down, fans shuffle out of the amphitheater. Sneakers and sandals crunch the gravel, kicking up dust. They're chugging the last of the warm beer from souvenir mugs and wearing glow sticks around their sunburned necks. It's been a long day of funking. I know I've got mere minutes before my boyfriend comes to rouse me and hand me a roll of cable. I lie down, stretch my back on a patch of damp grass and look up at the sky. Clouds have rolled in, and I can't see the stars, but I know they are there, and I picture them twinkling above the gray veil.

I see the boy in the Batman shirt, now in his father's arms, resting his head on his shoulder. The mother walks behind carrying the bag of toys. The boy is tired and is sucking his fingers, eyes drooping heavily. It's been a long day of learning.

# 12

# MERSA AND THE CANNIBAL

From the beginning Evan wanted to eat the girl's tragedies, to gorge himself on her pain. He wanted her body, of course he wanted her body, but that wasn't the main draw. He skimmed past her full v-neck sweater, hardly noticed her sharp, kittenish teeth, for he focused his hunger at the corner of her eye where her great sadness lay. The horizon of her mouth tipped up into a smile, but where the creases of her brow and eyelashes met, the skin folded down into a frown.

"Is this seat taken?" he asked, examining the crepe paper lines around her upper lip, thinking onion skin and layers.

The girl smiled, showing her teeth and a bit of gum. Her face brightened, and it was this light that led her girlfriends to call her 'perky,' but Evan saw beneath it. Her gums were puffed. From excess drugs? Too tired to floss? It didn't matter. He loved her. He had to have her.

Her wrists were so thin and delicate that Evan thought that if he'd wanted to, he could break her bone over his knees, snap her radius like a twig. This gave him an instant impulse to grab each side of her shoulder and squeeze until ten little bruise marks appeared beneath his ten square fingers. He imagined the bruises showing, just a bit, a little tease, beneath her sheer, white blouse.

Immediately though, Evan's stomach grew sour, and he had an urge to comfort her from his imaginary abuse. He reached out to touch her hair but stopped himself short and instead, tucked his own long hair behind his ears.

The girl fluttered her eyes, looked at him as if she knew what he was thinking, but she couldn't possibly have or else she wouldn't have moved her bag and patted the seat beside her.

Evan moved to accept the invitation, but his body was imbalanced--the right side of his body being slightly larger (bigger boned by a full inch around his wrist) so that when the train turned a bend, he lost his balance and slid towards the girl and brushed the side of his jeans across her face. A stylish rivet scraped her cheek and ripped a seam in her skin that extended from her hollow cheekbone all the way down to her chin. When he saw a swath of blood pool to the surface, something in his groin trilled.

"Oh God, I'm so sorry," he said as he lowered into the seat opposite her. He hadn't meant it, by god he hadn't, but the gruesome zipper of torn skin made the soft, white porcelain of her face glow with perfection.

So he cupped her chin and said, "I want to keep you safe."

She giggled, and a drop of blood landed on his second knuckle. He watched as it seeped into the tiny folds of his finger, spreading like a thousand red rivers.

The girl said, "I more fear what is within me than what comes from without."

It was the first words she had spoken to him, and Evan thought about the queer cadence to her voice and how the words sounded backwards. He pondered these things, but he did not want to hurt her feelings, so he kept his thoughts inside.

He looked over the girl's shoulder and watched as they passed a farm with placid cows lazily chewing their cud. Children's toys lay abandoned in the yard. An orange cat hunted for something in the clipped grass.

Evan listened to the rhythm of the track, watched the way the train shook and moved the girl's body with her relaxed consent. Her breasts shimmied loosely, her body in compliance with the train. Evan wished that he himself were a train because then he'd have the power to rock and soothe this girl into obedience.

Such a lusty thought made him feel vulnerable and small; it wasn't right. So, he obsessed about the girl's odd choice of words until his guilt subsided. His desire to correct her soon became greater than his desire to protect her.

You should have said, "I'm more afraid of what's within me than what comes from outside of me."

She cocked her head, and a flake of skin from around her eye floated down past her gash, past her lips and her chin and landed softly on her shoulder. His eye fixed on this small, vulnerable bit of her. It emboldened him, and he brushed the peel from her shoulder. The girl blinked again.

"The words are out of order, see?"

"What is order?" she asked, and he mistook her for stupid.

The train rocked along its track, rumbling like a bowling ball, jerking the girl's body towards the boy, away from the boy, towards the boy again, then away, her breasts lilting back and forth like a rocking horse. She was getting sleepy. He was gaining strength.

"What is your name?" he asked, and the girl told him.

"Mersa," and as she said this, a slip of skin pulled away from her lip.

Evan scrunched his brow and bit his lip, turned his head sideways and looked at her.

"No," he said. "That's not the right name for you."

"It isn't?" she said, the rectangle of skin lifting and lowering with her breath.

"Nope, not at all."

"That is my great grandmother's name, "she said.

"It's a drifter's name," Evan said.

Mersa looked him square in the eye.

"Precisely," she said. "I consider it an honor to house it," she said, and her eyes momentarily lost their sadness.

Evan was bothered by the motion of the chapped lip, and reaching over towards her mouth said, "May I?"

Mersa nodded. Evan grasped the skin between the short, square nails of his thumb and middle finger and pulled. Healthy skin came with it in a long, narrow strip, and now there was fresh blood an inch long along her mouth.

"Ouch!" Mersa said, bringing those slender, breakable fingers to her lips.

Evan hadn't meant to hurt her, and he said so.

"You told me I could do it," he said.

Mersa nodded, and another flake of skin peeled back from her thumb. With a small puff, she blew it towards the boy, and it landed on the crease of his eye. Evan blinked.

Evan rolled the lip skin between his fingers, turned it into a hard stone and flicked it into the aisle. Her pale eyes rimmed with water.

"Still, I'd like you to be more careful," she said.

The pain activated the perspiration under her arms, and he smelled her deodorant. This shamed Evan, so he was relieved when she turned her face to look out the window. Now, he could only look at the scratch and the tender side of her lip when she turned to face him.

"I didn't mean it," he said. "I'm clumsy. Haven't I been friendly to you since I got on?"

"I suppose you have," Mersa said.

"Didn't I ask you if I could sit down?"

All Mersa could do was nod.

She tapped her fingers lightly at the scratch on her cheek. It had begun to scab over, and bits of crust crumbled from the wound.

Evan looked over the girl's shoulder and saw that they were approaching a tunnel.

"How about me and you go out sometime after we get off this train?" he asked her.

She shuddered, and the light in the train car went dark.

But then Mersa smelled the boy's nice cologne. She felt the male-ness of his body as it rocked next to hers in the dark. When she sat next to him, she felt the smallness of her wrists, the teeny-ness of her own ears and lips and nose. In the dark, she intuited the clumsy and grand nature of his left side and sensed the soft, warmth of his finer right. She sensed him and knew him, took his sadness to heart. It was her mother's fault for naming her Mersa.

"OK," she said.

"OK," he said.

He searched for her in the dark, and his right hand found the tender spot beneath her ear and neck and pulled her towards him with his more delicate arm. Mersa, led by his gentleness, came forward to meet him. They bumped toward each other in the dark, and after a few misses to the cheek (his too far to the right, hers too far low) their lips met. Mersa felt the warmth of his mouth. Evan felt her open for him, and they both pressed in, tumbling in the dark toward each other, and Mersa's earrings jingled in their finding.

Mersa loved him too then, and her heart thought to break for him in this moment, and she let a tear escape from her eye. The tear dripped down her cheek and on to Evan's lip. He tasted the salt, and like the scent of blood excites a shark, Evan roused. Her vulnerability, her smallness. Her injury at his hand incited him, and Evan began to bite. First, gentle, playful nips, at which Mersa giggled and teased back. Encouraged, he took her bottom lip between his teeth and began to tug and pull. When Mersa began to pull back, Evan growled, bit down harder and shook his head side to side like her pet spaniel used to play with his chew toy.

"Ouch," she said, her lip still held captive by teeth, so her tongue had to do most of the work.

"I love you," he said, and he meant it.

Mersa wriggled her lip free from his mouth. Evan felt her slip away from him.

"Love is a temporary madness," Mersa said.

Mersa watched her blood pool in the corner of Evan's mouth. It began to boil on his lip.

"Talk plainly," he said, and his brows pinched together.

Her words always made him angry.

Evan's breath grew coarse, and his left arm began to grab at her hair. Even his feminine arm began to pinch and pull at her bra. They wrestled in the dark. Bits of her skin peeled off in layers along with her sweater, her bra, even the necklace around her throat that he kept in the tight grip of his palm. A corner of her ear fell with a wet thud onto the seat, and when the train car lurched, it rolled on to the grooved, rubber flooring of the train where it sat like a piece of dried fruit gathering bits of dirt and hair and dust. She reached out to grab it, but Evan pulled her hand to her heart. She felt it beating beneath her palm.

"Haven't I told you I love you?" he asked.

His urgency and desperation convinced her.

"Yes," she nodded. "Yes."

She was flattered. She was terrified. Evan went back to kneading at her body, pulling at her hair to expose her neck. He marked her throat with his kisses, broke buttons off her blouse with his clumsy hands. He thought he was saving her.

When he tugged at her jeans, she said firmly, "No."

"Yes," he said.

"No," she said.

He put his hand to the scrape on her cheek, stroked gently the missing skin on her lip, kissed the bit of her thumb. He touched at her wounds and scars, and this reminded Mersa of how small she was. Evan rubbed her body, stirring up the layers of her loose skin, sloughing it off until there wasn't a place on her that wasn't raw, tender and pink. Still, he scratched and scratched and her arms got thinner, and her thighs got thinner, and the hollow of her cheeks grew sallow. He thought he was making her new.

"My little gypsy," he said.

"Ouch," she said.

"I love you," he said. "Let me love you."

"But it hurts," she said

"Lift up," he said, tugging again at her jeans. "I'm not going to hurt you," he said. "I'm here to protect you. You can lean on me; you can stand on me. I will be your pillar."

She felt the hair of his left arm tease at her nipple. She wanted a pillar to stand on. She lifted up, and he wrestled her pants down to her knees.

"I will protect these delicate little arms."

She wanted protection.

He nibbled at her wrist, and a chunk of flesh caught in his mouth. He chewed and swallowed, her meat now inside of his stomach.

"I'll get in between you and harm," he said.

She wanted someone to stand in the gap.

He nibbled off a pinkie finger.

"I will die saving you."

She wanted saving.

Evan ate her ring finger next, and Mersa frowned for there was nowhere for him to display his promise. He pushed himself inside of her, and Mersa began to cry. Evan licked at her tears, his tongue scraping more skin off of her body, rolling the flesh upward like a jellyroll.

"There, there," he said, grunting and moving his hips.

"Didn't I ask you nicely?"

He pushed.

"And didn't you do what I asked?"

Mersa nodded as her layers unraveled. Centimeters and inches of her flesh came undone.

"You're hurting me," Mersa said.

"You're as much to blame," he said.

Mersa burned inside. She boiled. They groped and tugged and pulled for two more days before she finally decided. Before she finally said her thought out loud, "I don't like you."

Giving voice to the hate empowered her, and she began to kick and claw at his body with rolled up fists.

Evan sat up, his erection melting.

"How could you say that? It's such a mean thing. How could a beautiful girl say such a thing?"

Mersa felt bad. Mersa felt guilty. Mersa felt like she'd done an unspeakable thing, being rude in the way that she had.

Inside, behind the guilt, a light of intuition spoke to her.

"Run, run, run, run, run," it said.

She wanted to listen, but Mersa was afraid to go. If she ran, she'd be all alone on the train, and how would she know her stop? How could she pay the extended fare?  But the voice within persisted.

"Let me go," she said.

Evan pushed down on top of her body, kissing her. He bit down again, and the top ball of her lip came off in his mouth. Mersa narrowed her eyes and baited him with the plump flesh of her bottom lip.

The train conductor walked through the car, pointing his flashlight this way and that.

"Hold still," Evan said.

Mersa held still.

"Hold your breath. You're breathing too loud."

Mersa held her breath.

"That man is out to get you. I'll get between him and you. I'll always be here to protect you, to help you."

Mersa heard the ticking sound of her dry eyes blinking. She felt one eyeball stick to her tacky lid and pull out from the socket. It landed on the floor quietly. It caught in the man's searching flashlight, and Mersa watched it roll past her bit of ear and disappear beneath the seat in front of her.

Mersa felt the joints of her body loosen, and an arm that had been hanging over the edge of the seat got hit by Evan's knee and fell onto the floor with a thud.

"Ssssshhh," Evan said. "How will I keep you safe if you keep making noise?"

It couldn't be helped. The more he spoke, the more she fell apart. Her leg disconnected at the knee. Her remaining foot began to lose its toes.

Evan began to panic. Evan began to feel guilty.

One toe. Two. Three.

"I love you," he said.

Four.

"You know I love you, right?"

Mersa nodded.

The fifth toe landed on the rubber floor of the train car. The smell of her sweat, oniony and sharp, wafted beneath his nose. Evan wrapped his arms around Mersa and promised her and promised her and promised her until Mersa broke entirely apart and all that was left of her was a small, round button of her blue heart, pulsing with a dim light as the train made its way through the tunnel.

He put the heart in his pocket, "Lean on me," he said to the button heart.

"We'll have picnics in the meadow."

Mersa pulsed a weak agreement.

"We'll get married in a small church."

The light flickered brightly.

"We'll share a house."

The light cheerfully shined.

The train passed by a city and stopped at the station. A blonde woman in a stylish suit walked by Evan's window. So fresh, so pretty, so strong, so bright. He took Mersa out of his pocket and looked down at her. He became disinterested by the way she simply lie in his palm, pulsing like that.

Evan got bored and poked lazily at the button heart. Evan got curious and stuck a pin through it to the other side. Having nothing else to do, he split it open like meat and ate half of it.

But then he began to get angry that she was no longer flesh, no longer a body, that even her light had grown to dim from his nibbling and gnawing at it. She was so opposite the pretty blonde girl outside the window with her shiny hair and vibrant life.  He squeezed at the heart to get it to respond, and the heart did respond.

It flashed a message to him

..-. ..- -.-. -.- / -.-- --- ..- /..-. ..- -.-. -.- / -.-- --- ..-/ ..-. ..- -.-. -.- / -.-- --- ..-

Evan was hurt. Evan was enraged. After all he had done to protect her, all he had done to love her. He'd thought to eat the button heart, to swallow the rest of Mersa whole. But something had shifted in him, and he felt nauseated at the thought of the sick girl who allowed herself to be eaten.

Evan sat rolling the heart in his hands for a good long while as the train moved on its track. The pretty blonde he recognized from the station moved into his car. He rolled the heart in his hands, staring at the woman, wishing to save her. He rolled and rolled, and her body disintegrated like a rubbed eraser until Mersa was no more. The blonde woman sat down, opened a newspaper from her briefcase and began to read. He saw that it was *The Daily Mail* when he preferred *The Gazette*. He didn't want to hurt her feelings, so he didn't say anything, until his desire to correct her became greater than his desire to protect her.

# 13

# GOODBYE, RAY CHARLES. GOODBYE

It's been four days since the doctor sliced off my left breast. A red, angry scar slashes across my chest, and they've wrapped me tight in gauze like a mummy, trying to preserve a bit of me for my post-breast afterlife, if there is such a thing. I suspect it may be a myth. How is there life after such a significant part of your body is gone? Either blown off in war or carefully scalpeled away in one clean cut?

I'm in bed trying to sleep. My boyfriend pushes his crotch into my abdomen until he's hard. He undresses himself completely, and I'm still in my gray tee-shirt I use for painting, cleaning the toilets, sleeping. He pushes my nude-colored panties to the side, doesn't even take them off, and starts pumping inside of me. A hot swath flushes over the scar where my breast used to be, and the spreading warmth feels like losing blood.

"God," he says, and I hear him sigh. Smell mold on his breath. "Think you could *do* something here? Move around a little? Something?"

He runs one finger over the line of my scar, reading me like braille.

"I feel like I'm screwing a corpse."

I push with my hips, throw my head back and moan.

"That'll do," he says, and he tugs at my hair.

As he comes, quick and violent, I feel like I'm being hollowed out by the dull edges of a spoon, a long, slow goodbye.

Now there's no time for a shower. I wash in the sink and put my greasy hair in a loose bun. I make oatmeal in a paper bowl so that I can scarf it down in the car on my way to work.

He saunters into the kitchen, naked, lazily scratching his chest. He has nowhere to be until his "client meeting" at 2 in the afternoon.

He eyeballs the brown sugar bag sitting on the table.

"Can you try to put your stuff away before you leave for work?"

I see a swarm of fruit flies buzzing around his five empty tall boys from the night before. I say nothing.

I pick up the iPad needing to message the boss that I'll be late. As soon as I hit the browser button, porn pops up. Skinny Asians with tiny tits. Not middle-aged women like me with one gigantic tit and one scar. No one in a gray t-shirt and slack-muscled thighs.

"What's this?" I ask.

I tilt the screen towards him, and there's a gif of a cock being jammed into what looks like a teenager's mouth. It's a short video on infinite replay, and in and out the cock goes, in and out. The naked girl is on her knees, and she's at it all god damn day in three second loops.

"I was thinking," he says, changing the subject. "You might want to think about getting some medicated deodorant. You've been funky lately."

I blink.

"And you snore," he said. "Maybe it's the surgery? I don't know." He shrugs in a boyish, harmless way as if to imply that he's empathetic, that he's trying to help me out.

I mentally scroll through a variety of responses, unsure of which one to pick that won't start a war, but I must have frowned or slumped my shoulders because he sneers at me and says, "Why do you always play the victim? You do yourself a disservice."

I don't know which is worse. The spoon? Or the knife?

In the car, I leave the radio off and think about why I stay. The answer I give myself is, "It's easier than going." I wonder how much longer I can do this, and I'm afraid it may be until the cancer gets me once and for all.

It's week four AB, After Breast, and though the bandages remain snug against my torso, I feel like I have all of my parts. I still give myself a wide berth when I'm squeezing past the men in our tiny break room, and I act as if I still have those gorgeous, plump, round D cups taking up space, giving me substance. My breasts have always gone ahead of me, blazing a trail, and in this male dominated sales profession, I felt as though they made me more powerful, as if they were my giant set of gonads, and I had out-balled and thus out-manned all of the men around me.

I woke up one morning, the summer before sixth grade, and there they were. They matured before I did. They preceded my pubic hair, came before my first period. Full B cups that grew to C's that grew to almost D's by the time I hit my freshman year. I stood in front of the mirror, turning this way and that, bouncing my boobs in my cupped hands, enjoying their weight, playing with the responsive bounce in my nipple. I wasn't ready for it, but I was proud of them. They looked like the tits on Cinemax dad watched when mom was at ceramics class.

Don't get me wrong. My dad was never "that way" with me, but there was a sort of pride at becoming an object of beauty like the one my dad admired.

At fifteen, I thought I should have been proud of them. I mean, they were amazing, but it took only one day in the school hallway getting them "accidentally" jammed with an elbow, poked with a pencil, bored into with boys' stares to ask for a compressing sports bra and bulky sweaters.

There are few women in this job, and now it makes sense that I'm being masculated one body part at a time. First the left breast. Four months later, they say it may be the right too. I haven't healed enough for surgery, but I will get it as soon as they give me the go-ahead.

I think my boyfriend likes what's happened to me. He likes it in the way a man will make his pretty girlfriend fat by making her feel guilty for going to the gym or encouraging her to eat the cake he brought home. If her gut sticks out, if she has an outbreak of acne, if she is unattractive to other men, for sure he has the upper hand.

Upper hand is a big thing for my boyfriend.

"Hey, Cyclops," he says. He's taken to calling me Cyclops because I only have one breast. He thinks it's hilarious.

"We have to get to the party later. If we get there early, then Chuck will have the upper hand."

"What do you mean?" I ask. He's on the sofa playing a first-person shooter game, so it's 50/50 whether I'll get an answer. He finally replies back with, "Isn't it obvious?"

I take an anti-nausea pill. My stomach has been out of sorts since the surgery. When I don't say anything, my boyfriend continues.

"It's the way that guy thinks."

Chuck is the guy he works with. He imagines that Chuck is always trying to one up him, but he seems like a nice enough guy to me. He invited my boyfriend to play tennis with him, and my boyfriend found a way to take it as a slam against him.

"Rich, snooty jerk. Wants to show off."

"Maybe he wants to play tennis?" This is a statement, but my inflection implies that it's a question. I respond a lot to him with questions. I bend my elbows in and shrug my shoulders non-threateningly as if to say, "But what do I know?" It goes better this way.

"He only invited me to beat me. Or to show off his expensive shoes."

He's loaded up Mario Tennis Aces. I presume he's hoping the video game will help his real-world performance somehow.

"Well then maybe you shouldn't go?" I ask.

This infuriates him.

"Shouldn't go? Shouldn't go?! Of course I'm gonna' go. I can't NOT go. He would think I was a pussy or something. Yeah, I'm gonna' go. But I'll ask him to change the dates." He'll go on his own terms. He chuckles at his own cleverness.

I want the upper hand too. I want to go on my terms, but instead of breaking up with my boyfriend, I get the second breast removed. After the second surgery, I think he got the ghost pain too, the phantom limb. At first, he would reach out for my breasts in the dark, his hands seeking the mountains of soft, warm flesh he was used to. Instead, he finds air and thick embossed scars, and after his initial fetish about them, his hesitancy tells me that they're now a turn off.

It's Sunday morning, and light filters through the blinds. When he takes off my shirt, he looks surprised at the pink scars, and I see him draw back. He's quit calling me Cyclops and has moved on to Ray Charles.

I flip through the pamphlet the nurses gave me when I was discharged from the hospital. They've made a lot of advances in prosthetics and reconstructive surgery that promise to make me whole again. I ordered the double mastectomy bra, and I wear that not only at work but around the house too. I keep it on all day and all night and slip it off only after I've crawled into bed and turned off the lights.

On my phone, ads pop up for swimsuits that include breasts sewn in. I imagine myself stepping into the special one-piece suit and pulling synthetic boobs up past my knees, hips, waist, until I jostle them into the correct place over my scars. I look at the styles, and while the suits have modern cuts, even bikinis, there's something vaguely old lady-ish about them. First, they're mostly solid colors, and the patterned ones are a bit dated, two years out of style. I feel this way about my boyfriend. I'm two years behind leaving him. Three if you go by my girlfriends' advice, and the guy down the hall from me at work who wants to touch what he thinks are my real tits.

The first time a guy ever touched my boobs, I was 15 and a half, and he was 16. He was a shy boy, lived on my street, and he didn't say much. One time I missed my bus after school, and he offered to drive me home. He asked me questions about myself, and he actually let me answer them. I know he was listening too because he asked me questions to clarify, like which part of Germany did I want to visit or what was my favorite kind of shell to collect.

I asked him questions too, but he answered them only briefly before he deflected back to me. I admit that I loved this, even though I had a vague feeling of how selfish I was being. I couldn't help myself. I felt starved, and he was giving me food, real food to eat so that I was being nourished and flesh could grow on my bones. I felt in a tangible way that I was forming.

When we got home, we kept the conversation going in the driveway. It was deep winter, and the sun had gone down by 6:15, and we sat in his dark car listening to the radio and our breath fogged up the windows so that we couldn't see outside.

I felt a million emotions at once. There was wanderlust, and I wanted to drive away in the car with him forever, rumbling down the streets with a man who was safe. There was fear. I'd never even held a boy's hands before, and I could tell that he liked me in that way. And there was a sadness about growing up that I didn't understand until years later.

But because I felt like I could tell him anything, I spoke the truth and didn't pretend to be body-hating when the truth of the matter was, I loved my boobs. I don't know how the topic came up, but it did. I probably blurted it out with no warning, no ramp up, because that's how I used to be when I felt safe, open and honest. I remember the look on his face as I described them to him, serene and calm, amused. If he had leaned in, sweaty and eager, maybe I would have stopped at my appreciation for them, but I went on. I told him that I liked that they were big and bouncy. I told him that I liked the color of my nipples, pinkish brown, and I liked their size, like little pencil erasers, and how I could make them wrinkle and point with a quick squeeze.

"Can I see them?" he asked quietly.

"Sure," I said, and without hesitating, I lifted up my shirt, and I untucked the right breast from my bra. I untucked the left breast from my bra. I let the band from the bra hold everything up, perky and bright. I cupped them from beneath and squeezed my nipples into a point. Without asking, he reached out with his own hands and explored the weight of them, tested my nipple's response to first his fingers and then his mouth.

"Wow," he said over and over again.

I never felt more beautiful in all of my life.

That was over 25 years ago, but when I think of love and of safety and of all of the places I could go, when I think of my boobs and the phantom pain is menacing and strong, I think of him. His name was Paul, and he too is a phantom limb.

Months go by, and I still feel a hole where my breasts should be. The scars ache, first in pink, then in angry red. If I focus on it too much, it becomes green with gangrene and poison enters. I look up Paul on Instagram. His account is private, so I click "Follow" and tuck the phone into my purse. I call the plastic surgeon. I make an appointment. When my boyfriend comes home, I tell him we need to talk.

He laughs and says, "That's never good news."

We sit on opposite couches in the condo I purchased before I knew him. He chews at his lip.

"You look pretty today," he says from the hot seat.

He looks small and vulnerable. His nose is strong and handsome.

"This isn't really working out between us."

I cannot help but add a question.

"Is it?"

His eyebrows raise in surprise; then his eyes harden. The light goes out of them.

"No shit."

I'm strengthened by his vulgar defenses.

"I need you to move out," I say.

"Why should I be the one to go?" he asks.

I didn't think I should have to explain that this was my condo.

"Do you pay the mortgage?" I asked.

He's already off the couch.

"What took you so long?"

I shrug and shake my head.

"I don't know," I say, and even though I don't feel apologetic, I say, "I'm sorry."

"That's an arrogant thing to say," he says, rummaging through toiletries in the bathroom. "I should be thanking you."

My ex-boyfriend stomps around the bedroom throwing clothes into a black trash bag. I hear his boots on the hard wood, the opening and closing of the dresser drawers, the crinkling of his plastic bag. He exits the bedroom and crosses the living room floor.

"Have a nice life," he says and slams the front door closed behind him.

I raise my head and look at the door. Everything is so quiet. The air feels lighter somehow, less thick. I hadn't realized how shallow my breathing had become. I take in more air in a long, deep breath.

"Will do," I say to the closed front door.

The phone in my purse whistles. I take off my prosthetic bra, and it drops to the floor in a heavy droop. I stretch out my back, touch my hands to my scars. They feel soft and smooth beneath my fingertips, and I memorize their veins. It still feels odd to have air where my breasts once were, like I know it will feel strange to lie in bed tonight, scent and blank space where my boyfriend used to sleep. I climb into bed. I smell him still on the pillows, imagine that his side of the bed is still warm.

He left a dresser drawer slightly ajar, and a slip of fabric is sticking out. I want all evidence of him gone, so I crawl out of bed to fix it. When my feet touch the carpeted floor, I feel lighter. My back is at ease without the prosthetic bra pulling me down like an anchor. I open the drawer, tuck the errant fabric inside, but I realize something is out of place, something is missing. I flip through the odds and ends, a pair of Spanx, a waist trainer, some compression socks. What's gone missing? Suddenly, it occurs to me. My ex has taken the swimsuit, the one with the outdated palm tree fabric and the sewn-in breasts. I scoff out loud at this last-ditch attempt to own me in some way. I imagine him now, put up for the night in his niece's canopy bed. He's under the ruffled bedding, caressing the breasts of the suit, nuzzling his nose deep into the cleavage, crying, "Goodbye, Ray Charles. Goodbye."

# 14

# PADDLE LIKE HELL

"Owning a silver Camry is like having the name John. So ordinary," I say.

"Mmmm hmmm," he says.

I'm not sure he's listening. He's looking across the street at a billboard featuring a half-naked woman selling perfume, but he locks his arms at the small of my back and draws me close. "Some people like to blend in."

"I'm going to sell the Camero and get a silver Camry," I say.

He nods.

"I think I'll change my name to Susan."

He nods again and laughs, a huge burst of air booms from his windpipe.

He's got wild orange hair and a wooly beard. He knows nothing about camouflage. He looks down at his tricked-out wristwatch. It's got a space for a round, analog face that'll tick, tick. Instead, he installed a digital Casio. Like a lot of things about him, it doesn't make sense.

"We gots to go," he says.

He's smart and exceptionally gifted with words. He uses poor grammar on purpose. He straps a multi tool's leather pouch to his belt. Snaps on black wrist cuffs and bangs his palms against each, straining the leather. He looks like a boxer preparing to get into the ring.

"Yeaaah," he says nodding, grinning, arching his brow. "Now I'm ready."

He's so damn smart, and we go round and round about which one of us is smarter. I say it's me. He says it's him, but neither one of us knows anything about camouflage.

We walk down the street, and he makes eye contact with the ladies. "Hello," he says. They smile and giggle.

We walk down the street, and I make eye contact with the men. "Hello," I say. They turn to watch me walk.

We're both incurable flirts. A couple walks our way. He maintains his gaze with the woman in the same way I lower my eyes towards my shoulder at just the right moment. We have them both hooked.

"I'm going to sell the Camero and get a Camry," I say. "I'm going to leave Pennsylvania and move to West Virginia."

"You do that, Babe," he says.

And he means it. He gives me oceans of space that I take and use. I fiddle with the top I'm wearing so that it covers my bra strap. It had wider sleeves, but I trimmed them thinner with a pair of scissors. Now my shirt doesn't quite make sense. But it goes well with his Casio watch.

We walk down the street, holding hands. God we're badass. God we're cool. Jett, yeah, that's his given name, puts on his sunglasses. I put on my sunglasses.

And then I say to him, "I'm pregnant."

"Is it mine?"

He really wants to know. He gives me oceans of room.

"I don't want to go to the beach this year," I say. "I want to go to the mountains."

"Yeah. Starfish and such," he says lazily. "Wherever you want."

He takes my hand and talks knowledgeably about starfish reproduction while using stupidly poor grammar. A shy brunette with short, spriggy pigtails walks by. He looks right at her and grins. She looks at me, startled, then back to him. She blushes.

I wait until she walks far enough away that I can't hear her plastic bag crinkle.

"Yes, it's yours," I say.

"Well, what are you going to do?"

There's a cop giving out tickets. I think about winking, but my eyelids are heavy and tired. It's too much effort.

It's 10:30 a.m. and the parade's about to start. People are lining up on both sides of the street. It's unusually hot in Center City, Philadelphia, and the tar on the street is warming and starting to soften.

"I'm going to sell my car and get a Camry. I'm going to change my name to Susan."

"You said that," he said.

"Like the Cake song," I said." I'm going to move to West Virginia."

Jett waves away a buzzing fly.

"You said that," he says.

"You should change your name to John," I say.

Everything needs an overhaul.

"But I'm not a John," he says. "I'm a Jett." He strikes the Heisman pose, knee brought out to chest, arms out front to block. Energy coils in his shoulders.

"And you ain't no Susan. Susan stays at home and knits while everyone else goes out to party. Susan's a knitter."

"I can be Susan if I tried hard enough."

"You can be anything you want to be. You just gots to be you, Arabesque."

Arabesque, yeah, that's my given name. My family moved to the WV hills in the '70s during the hippie movement. They dug out their own latrines and planted soybeans before it was hip. I find myself craving endive salad and outhouses.

We reach a clear part of the curb along the parade route and sit. The concrete is warm from the sun. In the distance, we can hear a high school band butcher "Louie Louie." A group of teenaged girls walks by with short shorts eating cotton candy. A family passes by. A little girl in a red, white, and blue dress carries a plastic American flag. Everyone looks so happy, but the city behind them is dusty and dirty and filled with car exhaust.

Jett pinches my nose. The ocean he gives me swells and surges. I'm getting seasick.

"What are you going to do?" he asks again.

"We should go to the mountains this year and skip out on the beach."

"Sure," he says.

I'm in a tiny boat, untethered and bounced by the sea. Nausea rises. I clutch my stomach.

"You OK?" he asks.

I'm stuck in the undertow of my flamboyant name. I'm drowning in his obnoxious lack of jealousy.

"Gimmie a minute," I say leaning back onto the concrete.

Jett nods and pushes the hair out of my face. The world is spinning.

Fire engines, shined and polished for the parade, make their way around the corner. The driver turns on the siren. Onlookers hold their ears and smile at one another. A little boy points a sticky finger at a fire fighter in the crow's nest, 50 feet above the crowd. He's wearing full gear, and sweat trickles into his reflective uniform. It's a piece of Americana, and I want a slice.

"She's a girl," I say. "I'm going to call her Jane."

"If you're going to keep it, you should call it Anastasia," he says.

He watches me with his pale blue eyes, and I float out past the breakers, beyond the orange buoys. My stomach seizes.

"She's a *she*," I say. "Not an *it*."

"OK, Baby," Jett says. He's so agreeable.

With his finger, he traces small circles around my belly button. My stomach is still flat, and there's little evidence of the baby inside.

"And it's too big," I say.

"What's too big?" he asks, frowning.

"The name," I say. "The name is too big. I like Jane."

Jett picks a clover that managed to grow up through the cement and leans over to tickle my chin with its petals.

"At least spell it J. a. y. n. e," he says, "and she could turn out to be a bombshell."

I make a mental map of West Virginia. I see its mountains, its glorious rivers running through deep canyons, white water rafters perched atop its white spray. I picture red roofed houses and children playing in yards, catching crayfish in creeks. I see the main street parades. The sun is bearing down, and everything is washed out in white. Dreamy. Ethereal. Out of the corner of my eye, I see Jane in a plain red dress and two beautiful braids tied up with clean, blue ribbon. She is holding the hand of a man in a dark blue suit with a crisp, white shirt. He takes no shortcuts, not even with his name, so I call him David. Not Dave or Davey or D. Jett is eating a corn dog now. The ketchup drips onto his jeans. Nausea rises, and I remember what my daddy told me about undertow. Ride with the current until you feel your body unlock from the sea. Then paddle like hell towards the shore.

# 15

# ROLLER DERBY DOLL

It's fall in Chemical Valley, and the leaves are clinging to trees. I've got Jacob's hat in my hands, and I'm holding on just as tight as the leaves, thinking that beyond the corner of the death of this relationship is more death. After the goodbye comes the hauntings, seeing his ghost in every corner of this dying town.

The real Jacob's sitting in his car talking on his cell phone, and I can see that he's laughing.

I pound my fist onto my knee pads, first the left, then the right. I hook a finger through a line in my fishnet stockings and tug. I'm a honey. The fishnets make it so. The string pulls up and up and up away from my thigh, an inch, two inches, three, a foot, and snap! A hole. This aggression makes me a roller derby honey.

I take a drag on my cigarette. I pull and pull. There's something satisfying about watching the gray ash grow long and increasingly in danger of giving in to its own weight.

I wheel myself over to his car confident in my roller skates. Music's blaring through his open window. He's still laughing. I roll up to the windshield, come to a sexy stop that Diabla Divine taught me last week and bang my palms against his windshield.

He jumps; the phone falls out of his hand. Jacob's a small, nervous man.

"Christ," he says.

He's bent over the console, looking for the phone. He's in a hurry.

I put my hand on my hip and look out across the valley. Lower-income suburban homes dot the hills. There's room on the lots for a patch of grass and a one car garage they'll use to store Christmas decorations and house the dog at night.

White smokestacks from the chemical plant are pumping out white smoke. There's a billboard visible from the parking lot that reads, "The white clouds mean clean air." I imagine the miniscule particles of methylisocyanate, the 8,000 dead in Bhopal, India, how they transformed the 16-letter word into the snappy abbreviation: MIC. And here it is quietly invisible outside of my track.

He rushes the phone to his ear, "I'm sorry, Babe," he says to it.

I knew it had to be a woman.

"Crazy-ass knocked the phone out of my hand."

He nods in my direction.

Now I know the name he's given me, and I imagine them in bed, talking. "Crazy-ass threw a glass of bourbon in my face."

She'd stroke his arm and say, "I'm so sorry."

"Crazy-ass busted all of my records"

The blonde would sigh and coo in his ear.

"Crazy-ass called me names, Crazy-ass never went down on me, Crazy-ass, Crazy-ass, Crazy-ass," and as quick as that her nose would be nuzzling his balls.

I don't deny doing (or not doing) those things, but she'll see why. I take another drag from my cigarette, and I nod. She'll see.

"Love you," he says and pushes a red circle on their conversation.

He looks at me, and the smile fades from his face.

"Christ, you're smoking now?"

I stand there blinking. The sky is so sunny, the clouds from the smokestacks so white.

"What do you want?"

I can't find the words I'd so carefully planned out and rehearsed. They were buried under my shame, or my pride. It's all become a jumble, and I don't know which is which. I've lost the ability to detect whether telling him how I really feel is a strength or a weakness.

"Christ, what are you wearing?"

It's the only question I'm happy to answer for him.

"Surprise," I say. I raise my hands behind my neck, bump my hips, and vamp. "I'm a Chemical Valley Roller Girl."

He doesn't say anything, so I lower my arms and wrap them around my chest.

"You said this was an emergency. I got off work early to be here because you were crying about an emergency."

"It is an emergency. It's my first bout," I say. "I want you to watch me jam."

"I'm going back to work," he says, and he's already put the car into reverse.

"Wait," I say.

Jacob stops and looks me up down.

He says, "What in the hell possessed you to do this?"

I decide to tell him the truth.

I chew on my thumb and say, "I wanted to be made into a trading card."

A local photographer had made trading cards out of the team. Red uniforms on bright green backgrounds. They had names like Vicki Vixxxen and Diabla Divine, and they had been posted and liked by everyone I knew on Facebook. It presented so sexy, so strong. An instant way to gain power when I'd felt so impotent.

He snorts. Shakes his head.

"Honest to god, you're certifiable."

I want to tell him that there's nothing crazy about it. What girl doesn't dream of being a pinup? Who doesn't want to be the object of a man's desire? Of a woman's desire? Or both?

I want to tell him these things, but Jacob stops me short by saying, "You're thirty-one years old for crying out loud."

The wind stirs, and the trees are tired. I can tell by the way their limbs sag like hunched shoulders. I can see that they're giving up. The wind kicks up, and all their leafy beauty slides from their shoulders. There's a pile of gold and crimson lying at their feet.

He pulls away, and water sprays from his exhaust.

The air smells metallic and cold. It lingers in my hair.

I head to the track. The girls are standing around stretching, tugging spandex shorts out of their cracks, ripping two halves of their ponytails apart to bring the elastic tight to their scalps. My mouth goes dry, my fingers numb. What in the hell am I doing? They'll snap my arms like twigs. Their promises that my bony shoulders will make the perfect weapons are starting to feel like a marketing ploy.

"Hey Divine," I say.

Diabla Divine's standing next to the vending machine eating Funions. She nods in my direction.

"Today's the day," she says.

The smirk on her face is unnerving. She'd come on to me when I first started the team, but she gave up too early for me to give in. I park myself beside her, and I can smell the onion on her breath. On her it's been transformed into something savory and delicious. In the background there's the hot pretzels, the nacho cheese, the slushies they sell at the concession stand, and trace amounts of MIC, but I want more of her breath, so I lean in to smell her.

A bang echoes off the side wall. There's a pile of fishnets, scarves, short shorts, legs, arms, legs, more legs pressed against the wall. The Diamond City Scream Queens are warming up, showing us what they'll do to their own team. I shudder.

Roach sees my fear and says, "It's a game. There's only 2 derby girls among them. The rest are dolls."

"What's a doll?" I ask.

She spits on the carpeted floor.

"They're girls just here to be sexy."

I watch two dolls ram into each other. They seem vicious to me.

I'm a doll myself, and I know it. I have no business being here. Roller Derby is empowering and glamorous, but it can only be that way if I survive it. I imagine broken bones, chipped teeth, how sexy I'd look on crutches or with a permanent limp. How that thing Jacob used to do angled on the edge of the bed would hurt my injured hip if we got back together.

Divine slams her locker door shut with a swift blow from her elbow. Roach does the same.

"Did you vote today?" Roach asks.

This would seem like a non sequitur but not if you know Roach. Her dad won a Peabody and has been on Bill Maher. I'm intimidated. Which is how I feel more often than not these days. Threatened in the body, fearful in the mind. I've spent the last three weeks practically sleeping in my skates, trying to read newspapers when I'm on the can.

Divine nods. I start to fiddle with my skates.

"You didn't vote?"

Roach is in my face. Funions are sour on her.

"I didn't know the issues," I say.

"You should've made it your business to know the issues."

I know about issues, is what I'm thinking. One of her issues is hyper-politicism. Another is that her shorts are too tight. I know Jacob's issues regarding his mother. And I know my own major issue as well. It's acute apathy for anyone or anything that isn't me. I'm trying to work on it.

"I know," I say.

Roach shakes her head and skates past me letting her shoulder bang into my mine. My shoulder blades smash into the lockers, and they rattle.

"Don't worry about her," Divine says.

She grabs my wrists in her hands and says, "You are going to kick ass out there. You've been training for months."

I turn anxiously towards the track.

She pulls my chin so that her green eyes and my brown are aligned. Her eyes are wide and serious. They won't let me look away.

"Stop that shit," she says.

She's looking at my nose, my lips, back up at my eyes.

"Stop what?"

"Your fear."

She nods sharply.

"In the rink and out. Knock it off and let's go," she says and skates away, and the only thing I can do is follow her.


It's the third warm up lap and my muscles and joints still feel stiff. My bones are brittle, and I know they'll break. I've got to think warm thoughts, hot thoughts, Jacob holding my toothbrush, scrubbing my teeth and smiling at me, showing his dimple, the scruff of his hair unkempt from being under the blankets kissing my thighs. These images appear like specters reminding me that there are an infinite number of layers of hell to fall through. Little death after little death.

The Scream Queens keep barreling through the gate and I'm wondering how many. I stop to count, and their bodies are blurs moving past me, six, seven, eight, but they're so fast, so angry, their sexy presence so big that I lose count.

The bout begins.

I make it two laps without touching or being touched. Avoidance is a good strategy. Just when I think I may have a chance of surviving, a hot pain explodes on my side. It's Achilles Hell's elbow in my ribs. I can hardly breathe and instinctively bend over. Karma Suture kicks at my wheels, and my body is thrust forward. I tumble and twist, swirls of color surround me as I go down. All I can see is the brown grey cement of the floor and the outline of my nose, which I can already tell is starting to swell. My skull is on fire. I want to lie there and sleep. My hands are splayed out in front of me and wheels come within an inch of slicing them off.

I make it to my hands and knees, and Divine appears behind me, hooks a finger into the belt loop of my skirt, and pulls me to my feet. I look her way. She smiles, and I see blood outlining her teeth. She spits and skates off. I want to vomit and retreat. I want to yell, "This is a mistake! I'm just a doll."

I make it to the exit, but Divine looks at me and raises her fist in the air. I can't leave the bout when she's looking at me like that. Her taut triceps flex in the air. Blood is dripping down her chin, and she doesn't give a rat's ass. She is triumphant, and I tell myself, "A few more minutes. I think I can make it a few more minutes." Again, I can't tell what is strength and what is weakness.

I decide that the only way to survive this is to step outside of it and make a choice not to care, to put my apathy to good use. I pump my legs; I imagine them as steel pistons and springs. I am not muscle and bone, I am brick and mortar. My exhale is white clouds coming out of the smokestack that is my mouth. Chemicals are coming from my nostrils, the white smoke, the MIC. 8,000 will die at my feet.

Divine whips around me from behind; she's lapped me now and bodies pulse around me, undulating closer and farther away. It's an organic rhythm, this coming together and moving apart. It's a beautiful sport if you give in to the mechanical grace of it.

I bring my arms far behind me, then back up again, I am picking up speed. My hair is a windmill, and the moving air in my face brings me energy that I store in my mighty thighs. I see a doll a few feet ahead, and I ram my body into her side. She wasn't expecting me, and she wobbles for a moment before getting her balance. Oh yeah, I think. Oh yeah.

The machinery is moving now, and my thighs are pumping in long, clean strides. I. Am. A. Chemical. Valley. Roller. Girl.

I hit Achilles with a sharp shoulder in the way they told me to. I duck low, ram upward. She's a true derby girl, and I watch her body absorb the blow.    I am immediately on the ground, and I feel my shoulder slide along that gray floor that I was growing accustomed to. When I stop moving, I grin and scramble to my feet. I work to catch up with the action, music blaring in my chest.

Divine is ahead of me. She holds her hand out towards me, wants to use me as human artillery and rocket me out at another girl. I'm confident. I'm cocky. I think, even if I die on this track, I would feel no pain. It wouldn't hurt my metal bones, and out I'd go in a blaze of glory.

Perhaps after death there are not a thousand hells, but a quiet, peaceful nothing. I'm always thinking about death. Divine? She's got life in her eyes, in her smile, her very lifeblood is over spilling her body, and it's in her teeth and dribbling down her chin. She had a baby last year, had enough vitality in her to create life. Her sister is holding her little girl now and makes her wave from the side of the rink. She has her baby, her sister, her life, her blood, and I have nothing at all to lose.

I'm racing around the track, watching these powerful women in their 20's, their 30's, some of the fiercest are mid 40's. A migraine is forming at the base of my skull. Shards of light blur my vision. The ghost of Jacob, taking on the image of how cute he looked in the back seat of his car, is calling to me with his 50,000-watt smile from the side of the track. He's pointing at the rink's exit, holding out a towel and an iced tea. I pass the exit. I'm going for another 2-minute jam.

Ghost-Jacob looks disappointed, and something about his pout reminds me of Jacob in his car today, that casket of a car I never liked. The silver Toyota Camry, it's the official car of purgatory. There's no heaven in it, and there's no hell either. I've escaped it in the nick of time, like a death bed conversion.

I'm thinking that after death does not come more death. I think that after all the leaves have fallen off the trees and winter has come, that there is life beneath the earth. The tulips, the bulbs are resting and readying themselves to burst forth in spring.

I launch from Divine's hands and careen straight into Jezebel's Knife. We knot together at the elbow pads and go down together. She hits the ground first, but I land with a crack, and my head bounces off the concrete. Black spots invade my vision.

Splayed on the floor, I try pulling my limbs towards my body, but I'm stuck on top of Jezebel's Knife, and I can't tuck in as small as I want to in order to feel safe. The vibrations of skaters behind me are droning in my ear. The world slows down, and I feel as if I'm under water or someone's poisoned me with an ether rag. The vibrations are creeping closer. I sense a pack of jostling girls right behind me, and then I feel it. A blinding pain at my calves. Divine, behind me, tries to jump over my legs but leaps too late. My calves are throbbing a slow waltz, and the pain meanders all the way to the base of my neck. The nerves of my body are tied together and tangled, like me and Jezebel's body.

Diabla Divine careens forward, and I watch her, flying face first towards the rink's sides. I'm watching her hands outstretched in front of her. I see her baby's arm held in midair by her aunty. It's hanging there so small, so small suspended in air, the aunty's mouth a round O of fear. It's like looking at a snapshot, everything frozen in time and space. How is it happening? That slow motion before death. Maybe I am dying too? I look at Divine, arms stopped midair, her muscles pulled taught against her fishnet stockings, her hair frozen out behind her, her baby's hand in midair, wheels bang against my calves, Jezebel's elbow jammed into my boob.

Then everything starts moving again and Divine's head hits the board, her neck snaps back, and she drops heavy and solid, straight down without moving a muscle. The thud. The snap of her neck like the breaking of a twig. The straight drop like a bird hitting an apartment window. The referee has stopped the game and is checking Diabla's vitals. He's wearing a watch like Jacob used to wear. Jacob. I haven't thought of him for at least an hour. I raise my shoulders off the ground. The previous record had been 20 minutes.

Diabla Divine lay on the ground, a little cardinal, feathery bird, hollow bones laying empty shelled on the floor. Is she breathing? I can't tell if she's breathing. Her baby girl sits in her aunty's lap. She's wrestled off her shoe and her sock and is sucking happily on sloppy toes. Her daughter watches the motion of the other skaters go round and round.

I have Jacob's hash pipe, the His and Hers shot glasses, and the Rumi book he'd bought me for Christmas all loaded in a plastic Kroger's bag sitting by my front door. I'm going to leave this town and head west towards sunshine, shake the dust of Chemical Valley and its MIC off my feet. Chemical Valley is number one in tooth decay. Number one in obesity. And number one in early onset bovine deaths. Upon hearing news like this, Leah would have chanted, "We're number one! We're number one!" But it's empty without her, and winter limps along. She rests next to the bulbs, lying low, preparing for spring. I imagine the valley and how it will look when I go. In my rearview mirror, I'll see the row of smokestacks belching out white, happy clouds.

# 16

# CIRCLE, SQUIGGLE, FREE

Day One:

My new boss gives me a test he poached from a grad school management class.

Number these shapes in the order that they are pleasing to you.

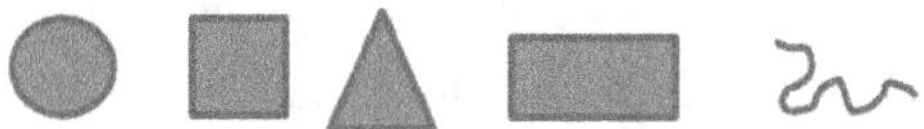

I pick the circle as number one and the squiggle as number two. The circle means I'm a nurturer, and I want to care for people. The squiggle means I am messy and don't like to follow specific procedure or protocol. It signifies that I am more of a free spirit who lacks organization. Squiggles are artists, and among them, writers.

I'm offended by this. I don't like being labeled in general, and I really don't like being labeled "free spirit" because this feels like code-word for "flake," and Appalachian women are not flakes. So I've decided to write down my day very precisely and specifically, like a square or triangle would do. Maybe in all of this data, I can figure out why I'm so restless.

Day Two:

6:20 a.m. I wake up my teenaged girls with a cheerful song. The lyrics go, "I know it's going to be a good day." I'm a terrible singer, and my voice cracks. They grumble. I sing louder. I click on their lights, bless them with my song. "Get the hell out," they say.

6:20-6:30 a.m. The girls won't eat school lunch, so I slice oranges, zip pepperoni rolls into plastic bags, guiltily drop Little Debbie's into each plastic sac. I'm feeling fat, so I put some grilled chicken and spinach in a stained Tupperware for myself.

6:50 a.m. I yell at the kids it's time to go. I yell. I yell. I yell. I threaten.

7:02 a.m. They get into the car. We drive with the door ajar light glaring because my youngest doesn't have the energy to slam the door hard enough to shut. Every time I apply the brakes, they squeak.

7:02-7:40 a.m. I drop the oldest off on the corner because we're late and don't have time to spend in the regular drop off line. She's angry about this, and when she looks at me, her eyes are powder kegs ready to go off, sticks of TNT at the mouth of the mines. She's resentful of the divorce, resentful that I can't afford $300 designer boots from Australia, resentful that I work late nights and can't chauffer her to and from her girlfriends' houses.

7:40-8:20 a.m. I maximize my time and improve myself by listening to an audiobook during my hour long commute out of the city and into the coalfields to teach. Today it's *Herland* by Charlotte Perkins Gillman, and it shames me deeply for sexualizing myself to please my boyfriend.

8:20 a.m. I ignore Gillman's message of liberation by putting make-up on in the parking lot. The $60 cream isn't working on my wrinkles. Skin sags beneath my eyes. I make a note to splurge and try the $120 cream when my adjunct money comes in.

8:20-9:15 a.m. I begin to grade a mountain of essays, but students come to office hours wanting to talk. Their boyfriends, laid off from the mines, keep letting them down. Circle side of me nurtures. I tell them to be strong, to get an education, that it's the best hope for being independent. In the back of my mind, I know I have a master's degree and two jobs, and I am barely scraping by.

9:30 a.m. to 8:45 p.m. Teach. Teach all God-damn day. Then drive to the night class while being audio-shamed by Gillman and teach. Teach all God-damn night. Stand in front of class with drawn on eyebrows and perform. Commas are sexy! Thesis statements are lit! We play games. I show videos. I do everything but get on a uni-cycle and juggle. They barely make C's on their grammar tests.

8:45 p.m. Pick up the girls. *How was your day?* They're tired and grumpy. They mumble while looking at their phones.

10:00 p.m. The 16-year old's gone to bed. I knock on her door. When she doesn't answer, I enter. Do I smell weed? *Get out,* she shrieks.

10:01 p.m. The 13-year-old wants me to tuck her in. I spread out each layer of blankets on top of her and stuff them tight to her body. I turn on her night light, close her blinds, fill her water glass. She wants me to watch a video. I do. It's of a boy she's obsessed with.

I'm glad she wants me to. She asks me to give her a kiss. We do Butterfly. We do Nose-touch (formerly known as Eskimo.) When I go to leave she says, *Tucking in is code for things I want you to do because I'm too lazy to do them.*

10:18 p.m. My boyfriend is happy to see me and grinds on me so I can't fall asleep. We start to have sex, good and pleasant, but now he's determined to make me come. His tongue is warm and soft, but I'm tired. I just can't do it. Too much on my mind. Add him to the list of people I've let down. I'm a bitch for bitching. I know women a decade younger than I am are stalking social media for clues that his relationship status has changed.

Day Three:

Same as day one and two, except I read an article saying tequila can fight type 2 diabetes and aid weight loss. I have a shot of tequila. Then another. I grade an A paper in front of the TV. Good Lord, it's an A paper! My heart sings. It's the 19-year-old girl with the two-year-old baby. Her husband is in jail for selling Oxy's. By God, the girl is catching on, she's catching on. Maybe she will make it.

My kids and boyfriend huddle around the Switch playing a game. They cheer and show me their score. They look happy. Relaxed. Tension drains out of my shoulders. I close my eyes, have no concept of dates or time. A wisp of euphoria slips in. When I fail to keep score, it's impossible to lose.

I clap and blow circle kisses. Squiggles float at the corners of my vision. I don't try to capture them or follow their path. I am tired of keeping triangle reigns and let my vision relax until the shapes are no more.

# 17

# BOYS BUY ME DRINKS TO WATCH ME FALL DOWN

I ordered a club soda and lime because I'd only been at this job two months, and when I drank alcohol, the outcome was liable to be unpredictable. I could fall asleep in 20 minutes, or I could get a second wind and get to singing karaoke, which I had no business doing. And now here I was at my very first professional convention as alert and eager as a young doe, not knowing that this function was one big drinking party and a hook up scene comparable to Tinder in real life, except instead of swiping right, all I had to do was glance right and see a potential match.

Anyone eligible (or not eligible) could make a high-class connection because this was a high-class resort, and I wasn't above pairing up if I met someone nice. So I got there early on the first day, left my luggage behind the front desk, and splurged on a sea salt scrub to make my skin pink and approachable. I practiced "falconry" where I could meet other bird lovers, which turned out to be an event run by an intern who released a blinded peregrine to fly 20 feet to a rotting chicken claw I clenched in my leather gloved hand. But it was all included with the resort, so I tried archery too. There I met a Bitcoin investor wearing very expensive shorts who, despite his repeated attempts, couldn't explain ghost money to me. I liked things I could see, feel, and rely on.

On that first evening, guests roasted weenies and marshmallows at a fire pit, and the teachers mingled with the high-end real estate agents, also on convention, and families trotted out children sporting clean clothing and fresh haircuts. Everything was so fancy, not like the Days Inn where the beige ceilings were tinted yellow from years of nicotine. So I was feeling pretty swanky when my coworkers caught a table at one of the bars that opened up to a patio overlooking the lake. The sun set gorgeously behind the mountains, and a crisp chill made the air feel thin and flimsy. Fog rolled in on top of the water, and the scene mirrored a painting from the hotel's grand lobby, and here I was living it in real time.

As the evening wore on, my cocktail facsimile became a mug of tea, warm and cozy beneath my fingers, the kind of thing a young teacher ought to be drinking at a teacher convention at a resort in October. Before too long, my boss and his boss, and my counterpart in the math department, began to stretch and yawn, and everyone disappeared to their rooms. But I was too excited to sleep, so I looked around for the tech guy I'd met earlier, but I didn't see him, or any potential mate, and I began to feel lonely.

In context, it was romantic. I sat alone on the Adirondack chairs watching the stars blink through the atmosphere, and I imagined my life as a rom-com in which my dream man walked up to me in white pants so sharply pleated that it cut through the fog as he approached.

In real life, the smell of woodsmoke and burned marshmallows wafted over to me from the fire pit, and an occasional laugh pushed out from the chatter. I closed my eyes and breathed in, and I felt my whole life ahead of me, with this new job and fresh haircut. I was thinking all of these hopeful things with my eyes closed, and I gave myself goose bumps thinking about how alive I was and how everything was possible for me at this time in my life.

I heard footsteps approaching, so I opened my eyes and saw a man in tan work boots, a gray hoodie, and loose-fitting jeans with multiple holes, but not the kind of holes the manufacturer put there.

I yelped and spilled some tea on my lap.

"Sorry to startle you, Ma'am," he said and shifted his weight to his back foot.

He had something in his right hand, a thin, shiny piece of metal, but I couldn't make it out.

"It's alright," I said, feeling a chill on my thigh where the tea had seeped through the fabric, and I kept my eyes on the glinting silver.

"I was wondering, Ma'am," he began, and his head was tilted down so he had to look at me through his lashes, "if you wanted to roast marshmallows with us?"

He moved his head to the side, exposing a little bit of his neck, and that made him appear unassuming, and

I recognized that the thing in his hand was a long, retractable roasting fork used at campfires.

"Now don't you worry. I'm not trying to hit on you."

His voice was deep and rumbly and reminded me of long road trips I used to take with my father. He scratched his jaw with the flat pad of his thumb and added, "I'm not like other guys."

This is the first time a man had ever said that to me. But in the years to come, I learned that every man that I've ever dated has thought that they were special in this particular way, and they all distanced themselves from their predatory peers. Some even let me behind the scenes telling me how other men behaved abominably towards women while reassuring me that they were above that kind of behavior. They spoke to me conspiratorially as if to say, "Here is the card trick, here is the magic. There are TWO girls in the box when the magician saws the assistant in half." When they wanted to lay it on thick, they explained that they'd been raised by single moms. They have sisters. They took a class in college called *Feminism and the Female Body*. How lucky I've been over the years to have met so many good men.

"You're not?" I asked.

"Nah. I'm just being friendly."

"C'mon. We're right over here. I'll introduce you to some friends of mine."

"Why don't you start by introducing yourself?"

"Oh yeah. Right," he said. "My name's Frankie. It's a pleasure to meet you."

I didn't like the "ie" at the end of his name because that marked him as a boy. He shifted the roasting fork to his left hand and extended his right for me to shake. I shook his hand, and then a dumb silence fell between us as I waited for him to ask my name.

"There's a bunch of nice people over there," he said. "There's my friends. A real estate lady."

He paused and added with a chuckle, "A mom drinking too much white wine."

I could think of a dozen reasons why a woman alone might avoid joining a bunch of strangers at a hotel fire pit. But there was something about the ritziness of the resort that gave me a sense of security. And then there was Frankie's exposed neck.

"Sure. I'll go," I said. "But only for a minute. I have a session at 8 am."

"Alright!" Frankie said, and on the short walk, I learned that he was originally from West Virginia, that he had 2 sisters, and he had a steady job and made good money as a construction worker and that he was here with his team for a convention.

"I didn't know that construction workers went to conventions," I said.

Frankie scoffed.

"We have safety trainings and whatnot."

I felt elitist for presuming that they had nothing to learn, and this made me apologetic and conciliatory right off the bat so that when he made a small innuendo about roasting weenies, I laughed encouragingly.

Once at the fire pit, I saw that there were also people from other colleges and some cosmetic dentists too, and we had a nice time exchanging small talk and stories, and when the mom finished her glass of wine and excused herself, I realized that I was the only woman still present.

"I guess this is my cue," I said, standing. "Time to hit the hay," and I slapped my thighs before standing to go. But Frankie pinched the sleeve of my shirt between his fingers and gave three little tugs and said, "Stay up a bit?"

He was doing that head tilty thing again, and he looked so cute, and because my dad built houses, and because my grandfather told stories to my brother and me in the dark, these men seem familiar to me, and maybe for me it was like how the bunny gets used to the domestic dog in the yard and doesn't run away. So I said, "Sure," and I sat back down. Frankie's chair was closer to mine than it was before. Or was I imagining that?

The foreman, Greg, was about 45, blonde hair, handsome and gregarious, and he suggested that Frankie get another round of drinks from the resort bar. Greg asked me what I was having. I'd been ordering Cape Cods in social situations outside of work because I liked the look of a pink drink and the contrasting green of the lime, and the cranberry really cut through the taste of the vodka, and when Frankie came back with a bucket of domestics for his friends and a Cape Cod for me, I set down my mug of tea, and that was the last I saw of it.

One of Frankie's friends flattered me by asking why I was hanging out with these ogres, and another guy asked what I did for a living, and though it's happened many times since, this was the first time a man confronted me with a few bars of "Hot for Teacher" by Van Halen.

"I got it bad, got it bad, got it bad," sang a guy from a dark corner of the patio. He wore a backward baseball cap and had small eyes that darted left and right but they were looking at nothing that I could see.

"Hey now," Frankie said in a protective way, and Backwards Baseball Cap Guy chuckled and leaned back into his chair. I felt mocked and a little embarrassed, but Frankie told me to "Ignore him," even though I felt him staring at me all night long.

Out of all the guys, Frankie was the closest to my age, though still probably a decade older at around 36. He was good about getting the drinks, finding napkins, going after the ketchup packets for the grilled hot dogs, and I liked this about him.

But it was late, and I was tired, and I yawned and gave a little stretch Frankie picked up on and asked, "You gonnna' be here tomorrow?"

I shrugged my shoulders, and Frankie said, "You better," and Greg and Backwards Baseball Cap Guy waved me off. I loved the sound of their voices rising and falling in the night as I walked away, imagining that I was doing it real mysterious like because I hadn't answered Frankie's question, and I had left them hanging.

In the morning, I learned about retention rates and collaborative learning, and it was a long day of sitting at round tables sucking on square resort mints, drinking bad coffee, but lunch and dinner were delicious, pan seared trout with fingerling potatoes, crown roast of pork with mushroom dressing, lemon cake with mascarpone. I'd never had crown roast or mascarpone. And after a complimentary sunset cruise on the lake and another evening drinking club soda at the bar with my coworkers, I was feeling fine. I thought quite a bit about Frankie, not as real relationship potential, but as someone I'd want to hook up with. Maybe? But by the time I had my second club soda with lime, I had decided ahead of time to go back to my room when everyone else went to theirs. But as my boss and I walked through the lobby at 10:04 pm, I saw Frankie, with his back towards me carrying one of those mini, blue Igloo coolers headed towards the patio.

I started in with the mental gymnastics I do when I'm trying to talk myself out of being good. It didn't take much, and I paused at the reception table to fill a plastic cup with icy, cucumber-basil water and said to my boss, "Don't wait on me." Once he was on the elevator and the doors had closed, I followed Frankie down to the fire pit.

I wasn't entirely naive. I'd had my share of awkward and uncomfortable experiences with other Backward Baseball Cap Guys who went a little too far, but I had forgotten about the wiener joke Frankie made within 60 seconds of meeting me, and I ascribed to him the role of protector. My approach to the fire pit was exactly as I had hoped. There was some cheering and some "she's back" and a grin spread across the entirety of Frankie's face.

"Let's get the teacher lady a seat," Greg said, and Frankie brought a chair over and placed it next to his, digging the legs of the chair into the gravel so that it set level.

"We hoped you were going to be here tonight, so we brought you something," Greg said.

The guys chuckled as if they we all in on some kind of joke, and I didn't know what to say. The gift could have been a pen from the hotel gift shop or it could have been a dick in a box for all I knew.

"Oh no," I said because that could have been interpreted two ways: 1. "you shouldn't have" or 2. "I'm in on the joke."

Greg held up the little Igloo cooler I'd seen Frankie carrying. He tapped the side before opening it up to reveal a small bottle of Tito's vodka, 16 ozs of Ocean Spray Cranberry, and one of those plastic limes filled with juice.

"We've got bottomless Cape Cods," Greg said.

I felt a prickle in my chest, a little firing of my intuition sending a warning shot, but all I could think to say was, "Awwww," followed by, "Thank you."

I downed my first drink within minutes. I didn't mean to, but on my second or third sip, Greg put a finger on the bottom of my cup and tipped it further and further until I swallowed the cocktail as I would a shot. Little trickles of Cape Cod dribbled out of both sides of my mouth, and I was ashamed to be spilling booze all over my face like that. Frankie frowned a little and handed me a napkin so that I could wipe my chin.

I didn't count the number of drinks I had like I usually do. But that's because I couldn't. There was always a refresher being poured, and my glass never emptied beyond half full. When I started to relax and my bones got a little floppy, Backwards Baseball Cap Guy crossed the fire pit, put his cap on my head and said, "You're our little mascot."

This made me feel very small, and a memory popped into my mind of a party in high school when a kid gave a puppy a beer, and everyone laughed all night at how it bumped into the furniture and howled at nothing in the corner.

This plus the vodka made me sad, and I wanted to go.

"I think I'm going to head out," I said.

"You think? Or you know?" Greg asked.

A screwy grin appeared on his face.

"Because I know you're going to stay."

If this were a movie, this is where a thunderclap would shake the theater, and the rain would pour down. A close up of my face would reveal my terror. I stood up to go, but the minute I left the chair, the world began to spin. I tried to steady myself on Frankie's elbow, but I fell over the arm of the chair and landed in the gravel.

"Whoa there," Greg said, pulling the hem of my skirt back down over my thighs.

"Don't wanna' give us a show," he said, but his hand patted my thigh like a good dog that had come to heel.

"Frankie will make sure that you get back to your room safe, won't you Frankie?"

Frankie nodded.

"I can get there myself."

"You'll be safe," Greg said as if he heard the alarm bells going off in my head. "He's not like the rest of us pricks."

Everyone laughed as if it was the funniest joke ever, and Backwards Baseball Cap Guy laughed the loudest.

"Thanks for everything. But I'm alright."

"You don't look alright," Frankie said, and he grabbed hold of my hands and brought me to my feet. I took a moment to rehearse the route I needed to take: Through the bar, up a small flight of stairs to the elevator to the fourth floor. Then did I go right or left?

I started to walk towards the bar.

"You're going the wrong way," Frankie said, and he led me away from the hotel.

"But it's this way," I insisted, and I was pretty sure that I was right.

"The bar closed an hour ago, and the doors are locked, so we have to go around," he explained.

"I'm sorry," I said. "I've had too much to drink."

"It's alright. It happens," Frankie said with great understanding.

For the first time that night, I saw Frankie smile, and two friendly dimples appeared. I started to relax a little and even got to feeling grateful that I had an escort. I kept thanking him, and he told me it was okay because we were on a pilgrimage, but I didn't know what he meant by that. By the time we stopped walking, we were nowhere near the hotel but instead somewhere standing on grass next to palates of brick covered by clear, plastic tarp.

"Where are we?" I asked.

"We're putting a sidewalk in here," he said, pointing.

"Aren't you here for a convention?" I asked, feeling like something wasn't quite square.

"Let's rest," Frankie said, and all he had to do was apply gentle pressure to my shoulders, and my back pressed up against the shrink-wrapped brick.

A few late cicadas chirped a weak mating call. Frankie wore an embarrassed grin.

"What?" I asked.

He shook his head no and chewed on his lip a little bit, shy and disarming.

"Why are you smiling like that?"

He sighed and took a deep breath in like I'd convinced him to tell me some kind of secret.

"I saw your panties earlier when you fell."

My tongue felt thick in my mouth, and I didn't want to be there. I tried saying so, but everything came out all wrong as if I had a mouth full of marbles.

"I'd like to see them again," he said.

I shook my head, but Frankie leaned forward and took hold of the hem of my dress and lifted it up and tucked it into the strap of my bra. His eyes twitched a little, and he wobbled a bit in his steel tipped boots. That's when I realized he was drunk too.

I pulled the fabric out of my bra and let it fall.

"Here. You hold it," he said, picking up the hem once more. The silky fabric of my dress brushed against my belly button, and it felt smooth and cool in the already cold air, and I thought, maybe if I did this thing, we could get back to the hotel, so I held it up for him as he got a good look at my body.

He stared and stared, and I looked down to see what he was seeing. I had been wearing plain, seamless, beige underwear that wouldn't show through my skirt.

"I'm sorry," I said and made some stupid joke about granny panties.

Frankie laughed, and I let my hands fall at my sides.

"Let's get you home," he said like I lived in the hotel. Like I didn't exist before the hotel and that I wouldn't exist afterwards, and that this was somehow my home, my place, the mascot with the comedically bad underwear.

Frankie got us back in to the hotel, and as we passed the front desk attendant, I used the tiled pattern on the floor as a guide to walk in a straight line. But once the elevator door closed behind us, Frankie put both of his hands on either side of my face, and said, "You're so pretty."

I swallowed and focused my eyes on the numbers as they went from 1 to 4, and Frankie kissed me on the side of my lips, like he had aimed for square center but had missed. The elevator chimed, and the door opened, and we stumbled towards my hotel room door, our hips bumping into one another as we walked. I couldn't get the card to swipe correctly, so Frankie took the card.

"Lemmie try," he said, and the door opened right up for him.

I stepped inside and turned around to face him, holding the door closed against my body.

"You are so tiny," Frankie said, ignoring my outstretched palm. "I'm afraid I will break your bones.

"What?" I asked.

"Like I could snap you right in half."

"Can I have my key, please?" I said.

He gave my palm a slap but didn't hand over the key card.

"I had a nice night, but I'm ready for bed."

"Let me get you settled," he said and pushed on the door.

It opened, he stepped around me, and my moment of big resistance was over. He sat me down on the bed and kneeled before me.

"Right shoe," he said, unbuckling the strap. "Left shoe."

He put his elbows on my bare knees and rested his head on top of them. He looked up at me, dozily drunk, his eyes big, blue mattresses.

"Don't break my ulna," I said, and Frankie laughed, but I was being sincere.

I felt Frankie's hand behind my head, leading my body onto the sheets, and I fell into a thick, cotton-headed sleep.

I woke up the next morning, my pulse throbbing in my ears. I was still in my dress from last night. My underwear too. I deduced that Frankie had dropped me off in bed. Maybe he kissed me a few times, maybe he hadn't.

I showered and did a double check and a triple check, noting that I didn't have that swollen, post-sex feeling between my legs.

As I downed some Tylenol, my phone pinged a text.

"How R U?"

"Who is this?"

"It's Frankie."

A blanket of dread weighted down my shoulders.

"How did you get my number?"

"I got it from UR phone while U were sleeping. U were pretty out of it."

I sighed. Pushed my palms into my eye sockets to make the headache go away. I wanted to correct his use of the word "sleeping" to "passed out," but who was I to say anything about it? That's not how a woman treats a man who got her to her room safely and then left.

While I was trying to think of what to type, he texted again.

"U wanna' go out some time?"

"I can't really do that," I typed.

"Why not?"

How could I explain that my appreciation weighed heavy? That Frankie's restraint was like a basket of crisp, new blue jeans and my gratitude a leaking gallon of bleach placed precariously on top.

"I just can't."

He was silent on the other end, so I texted again.

"But thanks for not being like all the other guys."

# 18

# STAYIN' ALIVE

As I ascended the small hill that was my driveway, reeking garbage bag in hand, I saw the curly top of a greying woman's head. The closer I got to the curb, the more of the street and her body came into view. Jowl-y neck. Comfortable jogger suit. She was entirely un-noticeable except that that she was holding on to an arm. She was grasping an arm, a thin arm, an arm enclosed in a cotton button down, the kind you might wear on a Thursday, not quite casual Friday, but you knew by this shirt that the weekend was getting close and soon you could kick up your heels.

The arm was attached to the torso of an old man. The torso of a man splayed on the ground. The body wore khaki pants and white, New Balance sneakers, and the woman had placed a pillow beneath the man's head. Now the woman was putting a jacket over the man's body, like he had decided to take a nap in the middle of the road, so cozy, the asphalt warmed by the late autumn sun.

The woman spotted me, and we locked eyes. She called out, her mouth pursing outward, then contracting into little O's, but I could not make out the words. She pointed to the man's body.

Finally, my synapses wrapped themselves around the sound.

"Cleo," she was calling out. "Cleo, Cleo."

She was slapping Cleo's hand and looking at me, her gaze like a tractor beam I could not escape, and she was pulling me towards her.

Up close, Cleo's skin was a thin, pale gray, his lips blue. My body shook with adrenaline. I was still clutching the trash bag filled with last week's rotting meat. I had crossed the street with it, and I had to set it down before I could place two fingers on the artery at Cleo's neck. His skin slid loosely beneath my fingers like an old, deflated balloon. No pulse. I placed my right hand on his forehead and my left hand on his chin. I pulled his jaws apart and looked inside. White gums. Silver fillings.

I stuck my finger inside his mouth, the rubber stickiness of his tongue ribbed and wet. No obstructions. I ran my fingers down the middle of his chest, the saliva from his mouth darkening a thin line on his shirt. I stopped at the nipples, clasped my two hands together, and pushed.

His bones cracked, and I felt the vibration of their movement between my hands. Dainty. Like a tiny batch of popcorn was cooking in his chest.

It's movie night. Cleo is making snacks. Cleo has become the show.

I pushed again. More bones cracking.

In training, it had all been a game, singing the Bee Gee's hit "Stayin' Alive" to keep time, making awkward jokes.

*Ah Ha Ha Ha Stayin' alive, stayin alive.*

Air hissed from Cleo's throat like compression brakes. I focused. Dropped completely into what I was doing, into the song in my head, trying to keep the movements as rhythmic as a heartbeat.

Cleo's eyes remained open and milky as if a ghost had already taken up residence, and I knew that if he were seeing, he was seeing somewhere else, somewhere out beyond his body. I kept right on pumping to that disco beat.

*Well, you can tell by the way I use my walk, I'm a ladies'*
*man, no time to talk.*
*And now it's alright, it's ok, and you may look the other*
*way.*

15 minutes went by, then 20, and my body spasmed with exhaustion. By the time the ambulance arrived and paramedics took over, my muscles were twitching so violently that I couldn't stand. I sat on the curb and watched as they electrified Cleo with paddles, as they draped a sheet over his body. The sheet as white as his new shoes.

At home, I could smell Cleo on my clothes, on my skin, in my hair. It was the scent of moths. Dusty. Fragile. Cold.

Deep purple bruises began to form on my knees. I fixed a Stoli and soda, the vodka leftover from a dinner party months ago. I took a gulp and turned it into a double. I remembered a joint I had saved in an old Sucrets tin along with my dad's cufflinks. It was dry and crinkly, in grave danger of falling apart the minute I puffed, but I was able to light it and inhale that sleepy smoke.

*Well now I get low and I get high and if I can't get either I really try.*

I had never before been this physically fatigued. Pain vibrated deep into my marrow like a wad of maggots trapped inside my bones. I remembered I'd forgotten the trash bag, left it in the street. I looked out my living room window, but someone must have dragged it away along with Cleo's body.

*Music gone and bodies cold, I've been kicked around since I've been born. And now it's alright. It's okay. I'm stayin' alive.*

I know now that there's no more intimate act than performing CPR. Not even sex. Or making love, if you need the distinction. You undress the body, you put your hands on the body, you become their breath. For days afterward, I felt like I had lost a lover, like my skin had dissolved and my organs were outside of my body, drying up in the air and the sun. I was parched and could not be sated. After that, I always had a glass of water in my perpetually trembling hands.

The second time I performed CPR was much like the first and only 8 days after Cleo Miller had died.

Older, white male. His ribs cracked too. I was on my way back from an office coffee run. I was thinking about the fact that I'd forgotten to order myself a drink and wondering what that meant when I saw a man in a blue wind breaker fall, clutching his chest. His wife, in a matching windbreaker, dialed 911, her mascara running.

"Don collapsed," she said into the phone. "Don Patton. His name is Don Patton."

She kept repeating his name as if saying it would keep him alive. The hair on my neck stood up. My stomach sank with dread. I held my cardboard carrier laden with drinks, and I waited for someone to intervene. With Cleo, the world had stood still. With Don, the world kept turning. Cars beeped. Hard soled shoes clicked on cement sidewalks.

Finally, I set down $48 worth of lattes and bent to check his pulse, but in my haste, I kicked over the whole thing. Coffee. The official sponsor of a new day, the drink of beginnings, now a tiny liquid river Styx heading towards the knees of my tights as I checked for obstructions. I unbuttoned Don's shirt, clutched my hands together, found the point between his nipples and pressed. And pressed. My muscles remembered the work. The place in my back that had been stiff for over a week lit up. The body remembers.

My tights split open as I continued pumping Don's chest. Legs and knees of bystanders pressed in around me. My elbows were bumping up against someone's shin, that's how close, and I felt my own throat began to close. When I looked up to tell them to give me some space, I found myself awash in a sea of cell phone cameras aimed right at me. This time, the EMT's arrived quickly, and I leaned against a thin windowsill and watched.

The paramedics zapped Don's chest in the same way they'd done Cleo, and they applied the same white sheet over his face. It's the loneliest feeling in the world, to touch a dying man all the way through until he becomes a dead man. No one came to speak to me, to ask me questions or give me some kind of de-brief. Not even Don's wife. I disappeared through the double glass doors of my office, coffee-less and shaking. I went straight to the water cooler and drank again and again from one of those little paper cones. I drank so much the paper gave through, and I needed a fresh cone.

The third time I performed CPR was a month later at my nephew's little league game. A woman in her 40's, Rene' Walker. She had the same color hair as my mother, brown with amber highlights. Rene' had Invisalign, and I will never forget the click it made when I removed the plastic trays.

The next day my mother called to tell me she had breast cancer. The outlook bleak. Had Cleo, Don, and Rene' been a sign? A way for the universe to acclimate me to my mother's impending death?

The fourth was two days after Rene', outside of Chick'n Out, my favorite place to get wings. Another man in his 50's, Thomas Carpenter. He had ordered his wings dry, and when he slouched to the ground, they fell out of the Styrofoam package and landed, sauce less, on the curb. When the ambulance left, I drank

Thomas' unopened Diet Coke that had rolled under the tire of a car.

Four times performing CPR, and four deaths to count. My failure was starting to get to me, my sanity starting to fracture. I had read that 9/11 rescue dogs got depressed finding dead body after dead body, so their trainers started planting live humans under steel girders and slabs of sheet rock so that the dogs could restore some amount of hope, a sense that their work mattered. I needed someone to plant a live body.

I joined Planet Fitness at $10 a month because by then, I began to expect people to drop in front of me, and I wanted to be more physically prepared. I attacked the rowing machine, isolated my glutes with the fervor of an ass model. I'd go straight home from the gym and drink more vodka, downgraded now to Smirnoff. I kept outings to work, family gatherings, and the gym and prayed no one in my line of sight would drop.

The fifth was a woman from my gym, Sara Wilson.

The sixth was a baby, Shyanne Edlin, a neighbor friend of my sister's who turned blue while sleeping in the shade in a pack n play at my niece's Frozen-themed birthday party. I can't say I wasn't prepared. I'd been watching videos on Youtube. Knew it would be inevitable that I would have to resuscitate someone so young, and I had been dreading it. How would I measure what force to use on a body that small? I left the party with a plate my sister made up and covered with foil. I sat in front of the TV and left the food untouched but sucked an entire case of Capri Suns I'd filched on my way out.

I began reading tarot cards to see if I could figure it out, and when that didn't work, I turned to essential oils, and when that didn't work, I tried Gnosticism in hopes that knowledge would save me. I jotted down the facts in a notebook. My name is Emily Thompson. I am a temp receptionist at the law firm Bailey, Bailey, and Burke. I like words on pages in orderly rows, especially law books setting precedents and guidelines to follow. I've never been interested in the medical field or social work, or any of the helping professions really. I'm shy, quiet, and I have a larger than usual bubble of preferred personal space. I started a new page in my journal and listed the following questions: What have I done to have earned this fate? What sin have I committed?  Like a macabre Groundhog Day, am I doomed to repeat it until someone finally, finally lives?

In Dante's *Inferno*, Virgil tells us of a man whose eyeballs are plucked out by crows, and once all the meat is out of the socket, the scene reboots. The man whose sin was lust once again has a fresh pair of eyes. The pain still lingering from the last assault, he watches as the crows alight on a branch. He knows what they are there to do, for he felt it merely minutes before. He hears their woeful cries, feels their little clawed feet land on his arms, their uneven gait as they make their way to his shoulder.

"Shoo, shoo," he says, "Please, please."

But he knows it will do no good. There are variants, of course. Sometimes two or three birds will attack one eye, sometimes one bird will take his time moving from the right eye to the left, drawing it all out, but the end result is always the same, and the show starts every hour on the hour.

I write down every rotten thing I had ever done for as long as I could remember.

When I was five, I wrote the word "fuck" in sidewalk chalk in front of our house.

When I was 8, I stole my brother's lawn- mowing money. He had saved up a whopping $50, and I was set with candy bars and gum all summer long.

When I was 13, I told my mother I hated her when she wouldn't buy me the dress I wanted for junior prom.

When I was 16, I told my mother I hated her for cheering too loudly at my softball game.

When I was 19, I allowed a frat guy to finger me in the bathroom of a college dive bar when I didn't even like him.

When I was 32, I told my mother, her chest bandaged at her removed breast, that I hated her because she insisted that none of these incidences of people dying in front of me were my fault.

My sister coaxed me into therapy, but I missed my first appointment because I performed CPR on the seventh person in the waiting room. Greg Jenkins, college professor, published writer, Mensa member. My second appointment, I performed CPR on my therapist, Nancy Reinhart. Before apologizing and rubbing her tingling arm, she reminded me of the statistics of CPR.

"Only 1 out of every 10 people actually fully recover after CPR."

After that, I refused to leave the house. I evoked FEMLA at my job, said my mother had cancer.  I quit the gym, told my family I was laying low for a while. I drank a lot of Popov vodka.

My mother, her head wrapped in a scarf because she had lost all her hair to chemo, drove to my house and cradled me in her arms. "I don't know what's going on," she said. "Maybe it's some kind of gift?"

"I hate you," I said, weakly.

"I know," she said and kissed my forehead.

When I had to perform CPR on a teen delivering Kung Pao chicken, my mother started leaving groceries at my door, knocking, and then texting me when she was far enough away to be safe.

My self-imposed exile didn't feel so bad. During that time, I paid bills online. Painted along with tutorials on YouTube. Ate meals that could be put in a blender and sucked through a straw.

And like any kind of detox, the pain of the poison leaves your body. You begin to think that you only imaged that you had a problem. That it had been one lone, horrific dream. You begin to feel normal again, and the strength comes back into your body.

Hopeful, I decided to walk down to the diner to get something solid to eat. I was craving pancakes with that ball of butter they form with a teeny ice cream scoop. The heated syrup would be extra runny and seep into the bacon. When I stepped outside, I was surprised to find that it was an autumn day (I thought it was summer) and the atmosphere felt thin and crisp. I wrapped my sweater around me and looked up at the sky. It was so blue, so razor sharp that it felt like steel cutting through me in a precise, cold line. I felt life all around me, and I breathed it in. A jaunty tune came into my head.

*Well you can tell by the way I use my walk*

The blue razor of light continued its movement within me. This felt novel. Interesting. Exciting. It snaked its way down into the left ventricle of my heart, and I perceived a new quiet, a new stillness in my body. I couldn't name it or recognize it.

. . .

. . .

. . .

. . .

. . .

. . .

. . .

. . .

. . .

. . .

. . .

. . .

. . .

. . .

These ellipses mark the passage of time in which nothing happens. Nothing at all.

Ellipses to mark the space in which I am living.

There is no such thing as time.

...

...

...

...

...

...

...

...

I don't know how I end up on the ground, but it is a clear autumn day, and it is my first day out in a long time. I am looking up at the clouds, white and cottony, and I remember the 5th grade Science project to glue cotton balls onto sheets of blue construction paper the shape of cumulus, cirrus, stratus clouds.

I'd thought I was too old for that, the assignment too fun and too easy to be of any use. Yet years later, I am looking up to the sky, and I know, these are cumulus with some wisps of cirrus to the east.

Why do I always think that the hard way must be the right way?

...

...

...

...

...

...

I put my right hand to my heart, and it is flickering weakly like a hose that had been kinked somewhere along a fence that I can't see. I should dial for help, but for reasons that I can't fully explain, the ache in my chest feels good to me, as if my body is finally coming into congruence with my soul.

I am on the verge of understanding myself, unraveling the pain that has been lodged for so many years, and it lay just out of reach like a piece of trivia that I once knew. Who invented DC current? Which vessel leads away from the heart? If I had enough time, I could remember.

And this is what it is like to come home. Or to have your demons come to roost. Or to finally forgive your mama for not being perfect, or to forgive your mama for being weak enough to get cancer. Or to finally forgive yourself for not loving her enough.

...

...

...

...

...

I expand beyond all four planes of existence.
Five, if you count the one where God dwells.

...

...

...

...

...

The sky is clear, the arteries are filled with sludge, the 5th grade teacher is giving you puddles of off- brand glue on a scrap piece of paper because there are not enough bottles to go around. The glue feels sticky on the tips of your fingers. Cleo Miller's breath smells like peanut butter. His fillings are silver. Your mama has lost her breast and does not look like herself. You dial 911 on your phone, but you pause before hitting send. The crow opens its beak but does not cry.

....

...

...

...

...

...

How easy. How easy it is to die. To let that mysterious electricity of the heart flicker out and stand in the park looking up at the sun, now sitting quietly on the bench. No, now lying on the grass looking up at the crystalline sky. Where has all the concrete gone? You can see the droplets that make up the clouds, individual atoms of hydrogen and oxygen. How easy to see when you float among them.

....

...

...

...

...

...

Why did I try to save anyone from such comfort?

...

...

..

# BOYS BUY ME DRINKS TO WATCH ME FALL DOWN

- 
- 
- 

# ACKNOWLEDGEMENTS

It is with my deepest appreciation that I acknowledge the following people, without whom, this book wouldn't be here.

David Scott Hay, one of my favorite writers, and definitely one of the good guys. Thank you for believing in my work and making this book happen. Without you, these stories would be on a thumb drive in my bills drawer and have never seen the light of day. Your feedback and edits were smart and insightful, and I'm a better writer after working with you. It's humbling to me that you were willing to take the time (so much time) and energy (so much energy) to help me grow my craft. Every writer needs an editor like you. Every writer needs a friend like you.

Allison Moore, I am deeply appreciative of the time and attention that you gave to this book and your willingness to put your good and talented name on it. You communicated my heart and intention in this thoughtful and smart introduction. It's a beautiful gift to feel seen and heard and given gravitas, especially by someone as gifted as you.

Miette Gillette, a fearless and badass woman who inspires me to be authentic. Thank you for taking on my book, and I'm honored to be at such an incredible publishing house. You've created something special, and I can't wait until all of your hard work pays off in more than just appreciation and gratitude.

Karin Fuller, you're my #1. I cherish the hours and hours we've spent talking about our writing lives and our personal lives. Without your encouragement and belief in me, I never would have had the courage to get my MFA, enter a contest, or even call myself a writer. Your expert edits (and lines you gave me) made my stories better, and in the process, you taught me craft. You're the real writer. I only take after you.

Judy Bodmer, you taught the first crisp and clean creative writing class that I ever sat in on, and your fundamentals stuck with me. Your kindness and encouragement can't go un-thanked.

All of my foxhole buddies and teachers from Queens University of Charlotte. I was lucky to be in pods and rub shoulders with some of the absolute best writers I know.

To Jeremy Rice, I appreciate your faith and belief in me. I felt that if a writer as talented as you encouraged my work, I could keep on going.

Robert L. Kelly, III, I started writing because you were a writer, and I wanted to be just like you.

I've been blessed with wonderful friends and family who have been ridiculously supportive of my writing in tangible ways as readers of my work: from Barb Panza who read the stuff I wrote in 5th grade, to Alicia Hall Bodden who was an early supporter and a careful reader of anything I sent her way, to Linda Dewald who gave her insightful feedback when it was down to the wire. Thanks to Jamie Lynn Crofts for titling "Rebound" and modeling authenticity in her work. Thanks to Lucy Manley, boss extraordinaire, for being mindful and kind enough to create a dream schedule so that I had time in the mornings to write.

Eric Pardue, I've admired your incredible artwork for a long time, and I can't believe that I got to collaborate with you on this cover project. By collaborate, I mean, slobber over your great work.

Brian Pickens, I love everything you do, and now that you've sprinkled your graphic design dust on my book, I couldn't be happier. Readers can find his work at Hashtagwv.com

*Anthology of Appalachian Writers*, thank you for reprint permission for "Circle Squiggle Free," Nikki Giovanni, Volume VIII edition and "Paddle Like Hell," Homer Hickam VII edition.

# ABOUT THE AUTHOR

Anna Dickson James loves helping young writers hone their craft and hosting online mastermind groups for women who, much like the characters in these stories, are seeking to level-up their lives.

# ABOUT THE PUBLISHER

Whisk(e)y Tit is committed to restoring degradation and degeneracy to the literary arts. We work with authors who are unwilling to sacrifice intellectual rigor, unrelenting playfulness, and visual beauty in our literary pursuits, often leading to texts that would otherwise be abandoned in today's largely homogenized literary landscape. In a world governed by idiocy, our commitment to these principles is an act of civil service and civil disobedience alike.

www.ingramcontent.com/pod-product-compliance
Lightning Source LLC
Chambersburg PA
CDITW060911210726

48293CB00006B/2051